How hard was it to say, *I'm pregnant*?

She sighed, and distracted herself by cleaning up her equipment and charts.

A strong, warm hand wrapped around her wrist and stopped her. She looked into his inquisitive eyes and swallowed.

"What do you need to tell me?"

She blew a light breath through her lips and tried to ignore the butterflies in her stomach.

He didn't let go. "Well, it's been exactly five weeks since we...ah...met."

"I remember it well. Now go on."

"And earlier this week, when I passed out, they ran some lab tests on me."

His head tilted the tiniest bit and his eyes grew more serious.

"The thing is...I'm pregnant," she whispered.

Lynne Marshall has been a registered nurse for twenty-five years. She's been an avid reader all her life. She began her writing journey in 2000, and quickly discovered Medical™ Romance allowed her to combine both her love of medicine and drama. Lynne is happily married to a police lieutenant, and has a grown daughter and son. Besides her passion for writing romance stories, she loves travel, reading, and power walks. You can visit Lynne's website at www.lynnemarshallweb.com

Recent titles by the same author:

SINGLE DAD, NURSE BRIDE
IN HIS ANGEL'S ARMS
HER L.A. KNIGHT
HER BABY'S SECRET FATHER

PREGNANT NURSE, NEW-FOUND FAMILY

BY
LYNNE MARSHALL

MILLS & BOON®
Pure reading pleasure™

First published in Great Britain 2008
Large Print edition 2009
Harlequin Mills & Boon Limited,
Eton House, 18-24 Paradise Road,
Richmond, Surrey TW9 1SR

© Janet Maarschalk 2008

ISBN: 978 0 263 20492 6

Set in Times Roman 16½ on 19 pt.
17-0209-47286

Printed and bound in Great Britain
by CPI Antony Rowe, Chippenham, Wiltshire

PREGNANT NURSE, NEW-FOUND FAMILY

This book is dedicated to the five years I worked as an allergy nurse, when I made special friends such as Joyce, Lorraine, Sue, Annette and Esther. With special thanks to Dr. Kenigsberg for helping me iron out my original premise, and in fond memory of Dr. Freund, a true gentleman.

CHAPTER ONE

THE last thing Gavin Riordan had ever expected was to be a full-time father again. The family courtroom drama had been legendary over the custody of his son three years before, but in the end the judge had ruled, as was most traditional, on the side of the mother.

He shook his head at the memory that Tuesday evening, and jogged down the hall in the clinic section of Los Angeles Mercy Hospital with his son in tow.

"Bupinder, have you got a minute?" He pulled the resistant nine-year-old, Patrick, along behind him.

The allergy doctor slowed down to let them catch up.

"May I run something by you?" he asked.

"Of course," she said.

"I tell you, it's the strangest thing." Gavin accompanied the petite allergist along the clinic corridor. "One minute Patrick was fine. The next he had a huge asthma attack. Got any ideas?"

Dr Bupinder Mehta slanted her head in thought and studied Gavin's son with large brown eyes. She turned back and asked, "Has he taken any antihistamines in the last week?"

"Not since the last big attack a month ago." That asthma attack had made sense, as his mother had been leaving for England the next day and Patrick had been torn up about saying goodbye. But why had he had the asthma flare-up this time?

They'd spent the day together and gone to the movies in the afternoon. Gavin was determined to make up for not being the father he should have been all along, now that Patrick was living with him again. As usual, as soon as they'd returned home on Sunday afternoon, Patrick had run to his bedroom and slammed the door. A short time later he had come out wheezing. "This last time he just needed inhalers."

"Then let's do a skin test. Pollens, food, we can do the whole panel if he's willing and you've got the time." She brushed her long, black braid over her white lab coat and pushed on the double doors to a large, bright waiting room.

"I guess there's no time like the present." Gavin rushed ahead and held the door open with one hand and scratched his neck with the other. He sent a glance his son's way and quickly saw the pursed lips and usual defensive resolve. He was positive his ex-wife Maureen's sudden departure for England for four months had something to do with Patrick's return of asthma after all these years.

Thinking of asthma as an emotional disease had been out of favor with the experts for a long time, yet Gavin still felt there was a connection. After he got some concrete medical answers, he'd deal with the emotional triggers in Patrick's life.

On a whim, Maureen had decided to take a university extension course in art history at

Oxford. She'd left Patrick with Gavin, even though it had meant putting him in a new school for the last few months before summer vacation and losing contact with all of his old friends. Maureen had always been impulsive, especially when it came to spending Gavin's money. Patrick was definitely unhappy with the situation. And Gavin was still adjusting to the added responsibility of being a full-time single dad while running the Mercy Hospital ER.

But he was determined to make things work. And right now that meant getting to the bottom of his son's new onset of asthma flare-ups.

"Beth, will you do one last skin test for me, please?" Dr Mehta's precise British accent echoed in the almost empty room.

The nurse snapped her head around and looked straight at them.

"I know it's late, but I'd like to do my colleague a favor, if you don't mind."

At first she looked startled, as if a spark of recognition flickered in her intense hazel eyes. She quickly recovered, and her stare washed over him like a cold wave. Holy smoke. She was the woman from the party.

"I think you've got the wrong person," she murmured in the hallway of the chief resident's condominium after the kiss that had made his toes curl.

"Feels pretty right to me." He tilted her chin and kissed her again. "My name's Gavin."

"I'm Bethany. Beth," she whispered over his mouth before smothering him with another brain-melting kiss.

Oh, yeah, she wanted him.

He hadn't used the best judgement that night. But he'd had no regrets. Not one. That was, until now.

She looked different with her hair pulled back into a tight ponytail, no make-up on, and baggy uniform scrubs, but she couldn't fool him. Though nothing like the wild woman he'd encountered a month ago, it was Beth nevertheless. She ignored him, while turning a deep shade of crimson, smiled at her boss, nodding her head as though no earth-shattering recognition had just occurred.

They were both adults. They'd made a choice to make love without knowing each other. So why did he feel so off balance? Because he'd never done anything as crazy as that before!

"I need to check Mr Plescia's arms, then I'll be right with you." She flicked her glance away before he had the chance to smile at her, and walked across the room to her other patient.

This could get awkward.

He'd hoped he would see her again, but he'd had to leave the party in a rush when his charge nurse, Carmen, had beeped and alerted him that Patrick had been admitted into an ER fifty miles away in Irvine with a full-blown asthma attack. That had been the Saturday night before his ex had left for England—his last weekend of freedom before becoming a full-time father again—and he'd acted like a crazed college student at a frat party. But, damn, he'd been angry with Maureen for pulling another stunt, and nervous about having his son come to live with him, and, well, he'd decided to cut loose. Not much to be proud of.

After the news about Patrick's asthma attack, he'd been so distracted he'd forgotten to ask for her full name or to get her phone number. It was an easy stretch to assume she thought he'd used her. In a way he had. He regretfully shook his head. Damn, he was out of practice. The least he could have done was found out where she worked and called her.

Well, surprise! She worked in Allergy, five stories up from the ER and located in the adjoining clinic wing of Mercy's large campus.

Patrick squeezed his hand. "I don't want to do this test."

"We've got to find out what keeps setting off your asthma, Patrick."

"What if it hurts?"

"I'll ask the nurse to be extra-gentle." The comment seemed to work as Patrick now studied the nurse with his pewter-colored pleading eyes.

The diminutive allergist nodded her head as she meticulously wrote on a green sheet and signed the allergy testing forms.

"Beth, do a complete panel and throw in all of

the foods we have. I know it's late, but I'll be sure you get overtime pay." She motioned for Gavin and Patrick to sit behind the patient interview counter. "I'll be in my office."

A huge blip crossed Beth's radar screen. This was the man from the party last month! His eyes had worked better than a hypnotist's watch while they'd stood assessing each other in the hallway at that resident's party that night, and she'd definitely been entranced by him. He'd felt so good pressing against her, good height, firm muscles spanning his chest and arms. They'd shared a first and second kiss as if a slow-motion magnet had been between them. And then…

After a sudden full body blush, her heart sank to her toes, along with all her blood. There he stood, arms folded, long wide stance, narrow hips, his sturdy, muscular frame covered in faded green ER scrubs and a white coat. And how could she forget his close-cropped brown hair? She'd run her hands through it countless times that night.

Do not blush again.

They'd made crazy love in a secluded room at the party, and now she couldn't even tell if he recognized her.

Gavin had looked surprised when she'd cut him down with her killer glance in front of his son, but that's what he deserved for not having the decency to remember who she was. It hurt to think she'd been that insignificant to him. But what else was new when it came to the men in her life?

To his credit, he did look a bit confused. Or chagrined. She should be offended, right? *He* had been the one to seduce *her*. She chose to ignore the fact that she'd been a willing and enthusiastic accomplice and had thoroughly enjoyed the whole experience.

He covered her mouth with a soft, warm kiss and teased her with tiny flicks of his tongue that managed to feather all the way down to her toes. She inhaled his steamy breath and parted her lips, tasting spearmint and spirits. And just when she let herself give in, he made an abrupt break away, a decisive look in his eyes. A firm grip circle her wrist. He tugged her down the hall to a room. A bedroom. Woozy from the combination of his mesmerizing kiss and peach daiquiris, she followed, knowing exactly what she was doing.

Intense, sexy eyes drilled into her when they reached the door. Decision time. Speak now or forever hold her peace. Beth hadn't felt this alive in years...

Her heart jittered with the memory. A quick reality check helped her realize it was time to "forever hold her peace". Some things were best left forgotten.

He hadn't even asked for her phone number when he'd gotten beeped and had run out on her. How cold had that been? Two could play at this game. If he pretended not to remember her, she'd do the same.

All business, she ignored Gavin and bent to talk to Patrick. "My name's Bethany. I'll be your nurse for the testing today. OK?" She noticed the purple and gold basketball jersey he wore with the number twenty-four on it. "Lakers fan, huh?"

The boy's eyes brightened and he smiled shyly and nodded. "Me, too." She took his hand. "Is this the shirt you wear when you need a little extra courage?"

"I guess."

"Don't worry, everything will be fine. Follow me."

She walked briskly toward the testing area, the boy's moist, floppy hand in hers, and forced herself to speak in a steady, soothing voice. "So what brings you to the clinic?"

"I dunno."

"When he was a baby he had twitchy lungs." Gavin broke in. "Then for several years he was fine. Now he's started with full-blown asthma attacks again." He looked thoughtfully at his son, as if they both knew when and why the new onset of asthma had started.

"I don't want to get tested, Dad." He squirmed, his face screwed up, and tears leaked from his squinted eyes.

"Patrick, you can do this, son." He gently put his hand on the boy's shoulder.

"Maybe your father should get tested, too."
She wasn't above stealth attacks.

The boy stopped protesting, and looked curiously up at his father.

Picking up on her suggestion, Gavin cast a wry glance her way and said, "Yeah. Sure. I'll go through it with you." Though he lacked obvious enthusiasm.

"The testing?" Patrick questioned in a high voice.

"Yup. We'll do it together." This time he sounded more convincing, and Beth managed to keep a straight face. Sweet revenge.

Patrick glanced cautiously at her. She smiled and lifted her brows. "What do you say?" Though Gavin did seem sincere, she tried not to credit him with any heroics. After all, she'd left him no way out.

An impish grin erupted on the boy's face, the first bright expression she'd seen from him since he'd shown up. His father nodded. "OK."

Pleased with her successful manipulation, she gave Gavin a cheeky smile. "Looks like you're on."

He blinked.

She gestured for Gavin and Patrick to take their seats. "Have either of you ever been tested for allergies before?"

Gavin stared at her mouth with a distracted subtle smile, while watching her talk.

Patrick's attention had been diverted to the television in the waiting room. As though on cue they both realized she'd asked them something. "What?" they said in unison.

"Pay attention, guys. I'm on overtime and we need to get this show on the road."

"Could you repeat the question, please?" Gavin's gaze drifted from her mouth back up to her glare.

Deep-set, molasses-colored eyes almost penetrated Beth's composure when she made the mistake of looking into them. Her mind went blank. An awkward staring contest ensued. Her breathing quickened. She cleared her throat. "I said, have either of you been tested for allergies before?"

"Never," he said, without releasing her from his stare.

A blush threatened. Beth willed it to stop, a futile endeavor. She ran a hand through her hair, wishing she'd fixed herself up a bit more today. Why hadn't she worn any make-up? Right, she had been running late this morning, feeling a bit queasy after her morning coffee. Obviously she'd made it too strong and her stomach had been out of sorts all day because of it. Come to think of it, she'd been feeling under the weather since last week.

"Dr Metha has ordered a lot of tests." She strode to the cabinet and removed two hospital gowns: one adult and one pediatric-sized—and discreetly glanced at Gavin's chest when she handed them over. She couldn't miss a soft patch of hair below his neck at the V of his hospital scrub top. "You'll both need to undress from the waist up. You know the drill, opening to the back."

He lifted his top over his head before she had a chance to close the curtain. A charming, boyish grin covered his face, though that wasn't where her eyes concentrated as he stood before her half-naked. She recalled how quickly he'd gotten undressed the last time they'd met. "I'm ready."

She wasn't. Beth couldn't help noticing the fine line of dark hair beginning at his trim waist and sprinkling upward across his substantial chest. She remembered how it had tickled her cheek. Her face went hot. She lifted her gaze and shot him a warning look for teasing her so openly in front of his son.

"Why don't you help Patrick with his gown?" she asked, distracted. "After that, you can sign these consents. I'll be back." She tossed the papers on the table and left before he could notice how much he'd affected her. But she suspected it was too late—how could he *not* have noticed?

"I'll be vaiting." His Arnold Schwarzenegger imitation wasn't half-bad.

She strode to the refrigerator and removed three trays of testing antigens, trying her best to steady her nerves.

Poor Patrick. Dr Mehta wanted the works and that's what the two of them would get. She'd get a certain satisfaction in stab— Er, scratching the cocksure doc a good sixty times in payment for being so damn sexy. But she felt bad for the boy.

It was never easy to test children, especially if they were afraid. At least Dr Mehta had come up with an abridged version for kids under twelve. Beth had been told by many of her patients that she had a soft touch, and today she'd definitely use it on Patrick. But Gavin? Well, that was another story.

She shook her head. So this was what she got for watching those chick-living-in-the-big-city sitcoms. They made casual sex seem so easy and without consequences. Well, here she was, sweating in her scrubs and wishing she'd never been so bold with the ER doc. What in the world had come over her that night? Two words. Gavin Riordan. And now, several weeks later, her total physical attraction to the man hadn't changed an iota.

She carefully placed the trays on a movable bedside table and rolled everything toward the half-closed curtain. Gavin, still naked from the waist up, swept the curtain open for her, affording another view of his muscular shoulders and arms. Everything about his incredibly superb physique affected her right down to the core, exactly the same way it had the night they'd "met".

"Here. I think you forgot this," she said, lifting the gown from the gurney and tossing it back at him.

Slightly off balance, Beth gulped and gestured with an unsteady hand toward the narrow gurneys. Making another attempt to sound professional, she concentrated on Patrick's scrawny body instead of his father's mature, masculine frame.

"I need both of you to lie face down on the testing tables."

"Now, that sounds like fun," Gavin said, obviously making light of what they were about to undergo for his son's sake.

Patrick dove for the gurney and it rolled a few inches, making him look like a surfer paddling out on the Pacific Ocean.

"Whoa, hold on, dude," Gavin stopped the gurney with a sculpted arm, and pressed on the brake.

Beth's gaze ran over the smooth tanned skin of his back. She shook her head. He was nothing more than a brief sensual treat. Eye candy. That's all.

An incredibly sexy memory of the two of them in a rather exotic position forced its way into her mind, and she almost lost her composure again.

Beth helped Patrick get into position on the gurney and gave him an encouraging look. "You'll do fine. I'll test your dad first, OK?"

The boy nodded in relief with a tense, thin-lipped smile.

She tried her best to ignore Gavin's goose-bumps at her touch, rationalizing that it was the cleansing alcohol wipe she'd applied, the potent whiff of which seemed to be taking her breath away...

Gavin felt Beth's breath blowing lightly over him. The fine hair on his neck stood erect and his skin prickled. She had a face he couldn't forget—bright hazel eyes surrounded by thick lashes and brows the color of dark honey, and a fine, straight nose. Her kissable lips were a natural tone. He'd already committed to memory how those lips felt. And her body. She'd tried her best to cover it up today, but he knew what was beneath those scrubs.

Where did they go from here? Hot sex with a stranger was one thing, but did he really want to get to know her? Maybe some things were best left forgotten.

It tickled when she drew something on his back and applied light, chilling drops of liquid. He relaxed and enjoyed the sensual feeling.

She began to scratch him beneath each of the droplets with something that felt like a needle. Hey! What was that?

"How does it feel, Dad?"

"Not bad at all," he fibbed. "Sort of like a pinch."

"Just a light scratch," Beth said.

Yeah, and we're just work colleagues.

Wanting to be a good example for his son, he managed a reassuring smile then laid his forehead down on the backs of his hands and forced himself to relax. But soon his head shot up. "I felt that one." Oops.

"Sorry. I was just thinking about the last time I saw you. A lady, um, called you away."

OK. So she definitely remembered him. Yeah, Carmen's timing had certainly sucked that night, but she'd found out that Patrick had been in the ER and had done the right thing by beeping him. It had been a much wiser choice than breaking in on them, though he was certain Carmen had known exactly what had been going on.

Ignoring another sharp scratch, Gavin seized the opportunity to explain. "That was no lady, that was my ER charge nurse, Carmen."

"I like Carmen," Patrick chimed in. "She lets me watch videos at her house sometimes."

"She was my designated driver, Bethany." He raised his head and looked over his shoulder. "What is your last name?"

Her eyes quickly flitted away. "Caldwell. Bethany Caldwell. Now, lie still or these drops will run together."

"Nice to meet you again, Bethany Caldwell. Carmen was supposed to keep me out of trouble that night." Gavin couldn't resist reminding her about them *meeting* the month before. Sure, he'd wished he'd known her last name and where she worked. If he'd had it all to do over again, he'd definitely handle the situation differently. It was probably too late to worry about that now, though.

"Did you get into trouble, Dad?"

"Nah, I was just kidding." Turning his attention back to Beth, he said, "As I recall, you're divorced, right?"

"My mom and dad are divorced." Patrick hadn't a clue what was going on but, as usual, just wanted to be in on the conversation.

Beth rolled the stool she sat on toward the counter to discard her cotton swabs and lancets. "Well, I guess we have something in common, then."

Gavin remembered her silly toast about her ex-husband at the party. Something about "May the dog lose his pecker in a mysterious accident." He scratched his nose and tried not to crack a smile. It sounded as though her marriage had ended as badly as his had.

She washed her hands and rolled toward Patrick's gurney.

"Now it's your turn, fella." She gave Patrick a

warm smile. Gavin liked the way she treated his son, especially as he missed his mother so much. He went back to resting his chin on a pedestal made from two fists, and thought he could get used to looking at Beth.

"That's cold," Patrick protested. "It tickles." He giggled and contorted while she drew lines and letters on his back.

"OK, let's get all the squirming over with before we start the test." She tickled his sides until he laughed so hard he relaxed.

It took a special woman to know how to work with kids. He'd give her that. Gavin optimistically calculated the odds of getting to know Bethany Caldwell better. He genuinely wasn't a cad. Not asking her full name or getting her number really had been beneath his usual standards. And never in his life had he carried on with a woman he hadn't even been introduced to. But, as they said, there's always a first. Hell, if they'd been dating and the sex had been that amazing, he'd have sent flowers the next day. But that night, with the strong sexual current flowing between them, his good sense had gotten left behind. And when Carmen had beeped him and alerted him about Patrick, well…

Now the question was, how could he make up for it?

Intense itching ratcheted up in wicked swirls around the test patches on his back. "Am I allowed to scratch?"

"Absolutely not."

"You're sadistic, you know that?"

"What's sadistic mean?" Patrick asked as Beth made the first scratch on his back. He didn't protest, but his face turned red from trying to hold still.

"It means she made my back itch a lot and won't let me scratch it."

"It's one of the perks of the job," she said, looking playfully at him for the first time that evening. He remembered that look.

Beth quickly finished testing Patrick without a peep coming from him. Gavin wondered why his back felt on fire but *his* son wasn't complaining at all.

"OK, guys. Now you have to lie here for twenty minutes."

"Hey, where are you going?" Gavin asked.

"To clean up the work station. It's closing time. Talk amongst yourselves."

He lay there like a good boy trying to be teacher's pet but his skin flushed from warm to hot, beginning from the top of his head downward. His scalp felt tingly. "Does your head itch?"

"Nope," Patrick said, looking very comfortable. "Hey, let's arm-wrestle."

Gavin cleared a tickle in his throat. His lungs twitched and itched inside. His beeper went off. He sat up. "Maybe later."

Using the wall phone, he dialed in the familiar ER numbers. "Riordan." He coughed while he listened, then glanced at his arms. They were covered with the beginnings of hives. Patrick's back looked pale, other than a few red dots and lots of writing.

"I'll be right down. Contact Orthopedics and the plastic surgeon on call." He hung up.

Beth reappeared at the door. Her eyes flashed

both a double-take and alarm when she saw Gavin. "Are you all right?" She glanced at Patrick to make sure he was OK.

"A four-year-old was just brought into the ER. I've got to go," he said, as the intense itching from his back spread all over his body.

"You can't leave. It looks like you're having a systemic reaction. And you can't leave a minor alone during skin testing. California law." She reached into the cupboard for a syringe and a vial.

The soles of his feet and palms of his hands joined the tornado of itching traveling across his skin. "They're waiting for me."

She wiped his arm with an alcohol swab and popped him with a needle.

"Ouch! Hey, what was that?"

Patrick looked on in alarm. "Do I gotta have that, too?"

She shook her head. "No, you're fine. But your dad is having a big reaction to the testing."

Patrick coughed.

"That was epi. Here, take this." She handed Gavin a small foil packet she'd torn open. "It's

an antihistamine. Dissolve it under your tongue."
She turned him round and assessed his back.
"Good God, a whole section of the testing has
run together into one huge welt. Let me check
your blood pressure."

"I told you I have to go." He coughed and
Patrick coughed along with him. Irritation accompanied his racing pulse and his lungs
wheezed. Tight, resistant huffs replaced his
normal breathing.

"Sit down." She gave his chest a firm shove and
angled him into a chair. "You won't do anyone
any good if you collapse in the elevator." She
fastened the blood-pressure cuff around his arm,
pumped it up, and listened with her stethoscope.
He flashed her an annoyed stare. Unfazed, she
bent forward in silence, almost head to head with
him as she listened to his blood pressure.

He started to stand up.

"Hold your horses. Good. Your pressure hasn't
dropped. Let me listen to your lungs." She placed
the cold stethoscope bell first on his chest then
on his back and commanded him to breathe in

and out for each. "I hear a little wheezing, but not bad. Let me roll you down to the ER in a wheelchair. You shouldn't be running around like this. And you can't leave Patrick alone here." She glanced at his back. "Man, you should be a bubble boy."

"Yeah, I've always been special. Look, this is ridiculous. I can walk."

"Maybe you can, but we don't want to spread this reaction any further by increasing your circulation with physical activity, so you're going in a wheelchair." She reached into the cupboard again and tossed him a small gray canister and then an aerochamber. "Take a couple of hits off that while I get the wheelchair."

He felt like an insolent teenager screwing up his face at a teacher's stupid idea, but did what he had been told for Patrick's sake. The woman was as pushy as his ER nurses, but he trusted her knowledge.

Before Beth left, she'd obviously become aware of what Gavin had been noticing for the last few weeks—Patrick's troublesome, persistent cough. He kept coughing as though he had a nervous tickle.

"Maybe you should take your asthma medicine, too," she said.

"I don't have it with me."

"Later, when we have time, I'll teach you about keeping peak-flow records and carrying your inhaler wherever you go, but for now, use what I gave your dad. You guys both need a bronchodilator."

She disappeared around the corner. Gavin heard her explain to Dr Mehta over the intercom what was going on, while they did what they were told.

Reappearing and rolling the wheelchair behind him, Beth caught the backs of his knees and pushed his shoulder down to force him to sit. She handed him his scrub top and lab coat and gave Patrick his basketball jersey.

"Would you like an ice pack or should I put some cortisone cream on your back before you get dressed?"

"Don't have time now, but I'd definitely like to

take a rain-check on the second part." Though nervous about his reaction to the testing, he couldn't resist horsing around to lighten her intense mood and help himself relax. He lowered his voice. "My choice of cream, though."

She lightly cuffed his shoulder and rolled her eyes toward Patrick. Ignoring Gavin's come-on, she spun the chair round and pushed it toward the door. "I'm missing dinner because of you, and I already skipped lunch today." With the clinic normally closing at five o'clock and it now being almost six o'clock, the hall was empty.

"Nurses are tough. What about our dinner?" He gestured to his son. "You know, I think you owe *us* dinner for all this grief."

"It was your idea," she said.

"Are we asking her to take us out, Dad?"

He grinned. "Maybe."

She ignored the implication and let Patrick push the elevator button on the fifth floor. Amazingly the door opened right away. She rolled him inside and stood across from both of them. Patrick punched number one.

"How am I supposed to figure out what you're allergic to if you're running around in the ER?" She fanned herself, looking suddenly flushed.

"You can't." Gavin studied his shaky hands. How was he supposed to examine a traumatized kid when he itched all over and his back burned hotter than Hades?

"Are you OK, Dad?" Patrick asked as he stood next to the wheelchair.

"I'm fine."

"It's just the medicine I gave him, Patrick. It will wear off. How about you? You seem to have stopped coughing."

"I'm good."

"The medicine helped?"

"Maybe."

Now pale and looking droopier by the second, Bethany leaned against the adjacent wall. "And why is it no one else can take care of this emergency?"

"Because I'm the head of the ER and the kid had his hand practically torn off by the family dog."

He glanced across the elevator just in time to see his new, and definitely favorite, allergy nurse fainting.

CHAPTER TWO

GAVIN punched in the code on the number pad of the emergency room door—it swung open to harsh fluorescent lights and a barrage of noise. Ah, home, sweet home.

"I need an ammonia ampoule," he said, acting like carrying a woman over his shoulder was the most natural thing in the world. Patrick followed, pushing the empty wheelchair.

When Bethany had started to fall, he'd lunged across the elevator, catching her just above the knees, and hoisted her over his shoulder.

With her usual ER charm, Carmen nailed him over her half-rimmed glasses. "Where have you been, and who is she?" After twenty years in the ER, nothing fazed her.

"This my allergy nurse." He made a circle, looking for a vacant exam room.

"Room three is open. Hi, Patrick, darlin'." Her icy glare cracked into a smile just for him. "You can leave the wheelchair right there."

Gavin headed across the ward with Patrick behind him, gently laid Bethany on the gurney in the vacant room, then adjusted the head of the bed so that her head was below her heart.

Carmen appeared at the doorway, arms folded, a curious look on her face. She handed him the smelling salts. He'd thought he'd save her the question.

"She passed out in the elevator when I mentioned the boy's hand almost being ripped off by a dog." Realizing his son had heard every word, he gave him a steady look and said, "I'll make sure the boy is fine. These days surgeons can reattach just about everything." Patrick nodded thoughtfully. Glancing back at Carmen, who was waiting for more explanation, Gavin said, "I caught her before she hit the floor." He popped open and waved the smelling salts under Beth's nose. A reflex made her shake her head side to side. "Keep an eye on her for me while I take a look at the boy, will you?"

"Sure. We've only got patients crawling out of the rafters and as usual I'm short-staffed, but I'll take care of her." Carmen approached the bedside and applied the blood-pressure cuff to Beth's arm. "Is this some new dating strategy?"

Patrick laughed as if he understood what she was talking about. Carmen's mock vitriol for Gavin disappeared when she smiled at the boy.

Choosing to ignore her smart-aleck question, Gavin said, "Patrick, you stay with Carmen and Bethany."

"The boy's in room six, we've got a GI bleed in room three, and there's a possible kidney stone in eight." Carmen's expression changed from all business to concern when she had time to study him more closely. "What the heck happened to you?"

"She tried to kill me." He nodded toward Beth before heading toward room six. Halfway there, he glanced over his shoulder. "Order an IVP for room eight, draw a stat CBC, 'lytes, PT and PTT for three."

"Already have, but thanks for making it official," Carmen spouted off confidently, making note of her newest patient's BP. "Hey, Gav, what about something for pain for the possible kidney stone?" she called over her shoulder.

He slowed his pace. "Any drug allergies?"

"None."

"Demerol 75 milligrams IM." A deep appreciation for his skilled and competent nurse made him smile. He'd left Beth in good hands. "What would I do without you?"

"Crash and burn," she said on a sigh as she headed for the tiny medicine alcove.

Beth lay perfectly still, woozy yet distracted by the noise and chaos. She opened her eyes and saw Patrick's inquisitive gaze watching her as if she'd died and come back to life. He'd been raising and lowering the height of the bed by pushing the buttons on the side rails. For a while she'd dreamed she was on a Caribbean cruise, rocking and rolling at sea.

"Hey," she said.

"Hi." He quickly moved his hand. "Dad said you fainted."

"How long was I out?"

"Not very long."

She sat up, fighting an uphill battle with the gurney. "Can you push that and fix this?"

The boy eagerly complied, already a pro at the bedside controls. The blood-pressure cuff automatically pumped up again. Her BP was normal. She sat up, feeling fine now. She knew she shouldn't have skipped lunch, but she'd still felt queasy and the thought of food had made her sick. And when dinner had been postponed, well, it must have caught up with her.

She glanced across the cavernous ER to another room. Behind the glass wall, Gavin was conversing with a doctor and a man and woman. A small boy lay behind him on the gurney. Her gaze came to rest on a teenage girl standing just outside the door. The girl chewed on her index finger and rubbed at red, swollen eyes; fear and concern furrowed her brow as she peered inside.

The timer on Beth's wristwatch went off. She'd set it just before they'd left the allergy department. "Oh, Patrick, it's time to check your back." She fished around in her pocket for her calibrator to measure any redness or induration from the tests. "Take off your shirt." She found her pen and a piece of scrap paper in her lab coat and, when Patrick backed up so she could see, began assessing the few small welts on his back. "Most everything is normal. You've got a mild reaction to grass and a couple of the trees. Oh, cat fur is borderline."

"What does borderline mean?"

"It means you're probably OK. Do you have a cat?"

"No. But I used to." He got suddenly quiet.

"Well, other than the grass and trees, you're OK. Can you get me a glass of water?"

He put his jersey back on and used the bedside sink to fill a small cup normally meant for pills. She smiled and took it gratefully, threw the contents back in one gulp and asked for another. "Do you have any candy on you? I'm starving."

He shook his head but just as quickly his eyes brightened. "I know where the snack machines are." Spoken like a kid who'd spent more than his share of hours hanging around the hospital because his dad was head of the ER.

Carmen appeared at the door with a lab tray.

"Oh, I'm fine now. I just need to get something to eat."

"You know the drill," Carmen said, setting her tray at the bedside and applying a tourniquet to Beth's arm. "You show up in the ER and we've got to do blood tests. I had Rick, the supervising PA, order them."

Knowing there was no getting around hospital protocol, Beth lay back and let Carmen do her job.

"Do I have to watch?" Patrick asked, his fine brows pinched together.

"If I give you a dollar, will you buy me a chocolate bar?" With her free hand Beth found a dollar and some change in the other pocket and gave him a handful. "Get yourself something, too."

He shot out of the room as though on a world-saving mission before Carmen had a chance to expose a needle.

"So what did you do to Gavin? He looks like Lobster Man."

"I know! And because he's running around here, I can't read his skin tests to find out what he's allergic to." She sighed. "What am I being tested for?"

Carmen was so skilled at drawing blood that Beth barely felt the needle pierce her skin. "The usual lab tests. Blood sugar. Electrolytes. When was your last period?"

Beth scratched her head and thought about it. Wait a second. Normally, she'd be having her period around this time, or maybe it was supposed to be last week?

Hesitating, she gave the information to her nurse.

Subtly lifting a brow, Carmen said, "Maybe I'll throw in a pregnancy test." She gathered her vials and left the room without giving Beth a hint about whether or not she knew what had gone on between her and Gavin a few weeks ago. Beth recognized her distinctive voice. But did Carmen know who Beth was?

The ripple effect of her poor judgement caused a second wave of lightheadedness, and forced Beth to lean back on the bed. Nah. No way. They'd used protection.

"Who'll get the results?" she called out, without thinking things through.

"Rick will call you if anything's abnormal."

She'd been in this situation before, twice. Hell, that was the reason she'd gotten married, and her husband hadn't been in the least bit happy about it. She hadn't done it to trap him. It had just sort of happened. Back when she'd married Neal, she'd wanted nothing more than to have a family, but after they'd married, she'd miscarried within the first trimester. A year later, it had happened again; it wasn't meant to be. Then he'd run off with that woman after maxing out Beth's credit cards. Just thinking about her ex and the bosomy blonde he'd left her for sent her blood pressure into the stratosphere.

Oh, God, what if she was pregnant? She'd

promised herself to only marry for love in the future, no matter what. Gavin was a total stranger.

To distract herself, Beth watched the girl standing outside the boy's room across the ward. She'd been working at the teen clinic a couple nights a week for the last year and, with her own memories of teenage angst, she felt she'd finally cracked the code of what made them tick. Drawn by the girl's silent scream and avoiding her own over a possible pregnancy, she decided to check things out.

"Hi," Beth said, when she approached.

"I belong here. That's my brother," the girl answered, with both shoulders raised as if ready for a fight.

"You look pretty worried." Beth edged closer.

"Well, wouldn't you be?" she barked, and bit at the hangnail on her finger, avoiding Beth's eyes.

"Oh, gosh, yes. But he's in good hands now." She was careful not to invade the teenager's space and remained a couple of feet away while the girl leaned against the wall. "Mind if I keep you company?" Before the girl could answer, she went on, "What's his name?"

"Andrew." The petite girl shrugged.

"Well, Andrew will get the best of care. The surgeons will do everything they can to save his hand."

"It's my fault he's here." Frightened eyes peered above her knuckles, tears slipped over the red rims of her eyes and down her pale cheeks. Her composure completely gone, the girl's shoulders jerked up and down with a new onslaught of sobs.

Beth reached out and wrapped the twig-thin teen under her arm. "It's not your fault, you know." She guided the girl toward a bench along the wall, away from her brother's room. "*You* didn't bite him."

"I left him alone when I answered my cell-phone." Guilt wrenched through a squeaky, gasping voice.

Beth took a deep breath, unsure what tack to take. "Was he a vicious dog?"

"No!" the girl snapped, then backed off a bit. "That's the thing—he's been our family pet for ever."

"So how were you supposed to know…? What's your dog's name?"

"Max."

"How were you supposed to know Max would attack Andrew?" Beth gently prodded the girl to sit down and joined her.

She sobbed into her hands. "Now we've got to put Max down and my brother's lost his hand, all because of my stupid cellphone."

Beth placed her arm gently across the girl's back. "Sometimes life just happens and we don't have any control over it." Beth sat in silence, giving the girl time to think while turning over and over her own thoughts about a possible pregnancy. "The doctors may be able to save your brother's hand. Just have some faith. My name's Beth—what's yours?"

"Courtney." She wiped her eyes and glanced at Beth.

"Courtney, it's not your fault—have you got that?" Beth squeezed her bony shoulder. "Maybe Max was in pain or he was frightened or he's started to get senile. Maybe a bee stung him.

There could be several reasons why he'd attack your brother."

The girl whimpered and nodded.

Gavin watched with an ache in his heart as the orderly wheeled the sedated child toward the door on his way to the operating room. Finally, the traumatized boy was calm and on his way to surgery.

Thick black lashes rested on the child's blanched cheeks, reminding him of his own son. If the doctors did their jobs properly, Andrew would have no memory of what was to come, and his hand would be useful again. Gavin made a mental note to follow up on the boy's progress later.

His gaze went to a scrawny teenager outside the room, wrapped in the comforting arm of his newest favorite nurse, Bethany Caldwell. She must be feeling better. Patrick was sitting beside her and they were all sharing a couple of candy bars.

Gavin liked seeing her in his department; he liked that she'd taken the initiative to support the forgotten family member. His own nurses rarely had time for such things. And she hadn't stuck Carmen with watching his son, as he often was forced to do.

His son suddenly being left with him by his ex had clearly turned into a gift—the gift of a second chance. He smiled, thankful for odd favors.

"Hi, Dad!" Patrick waved from across the room, content to hang around until he could go home. His heart squeezed. What a trouper. The way things were going, he'd be stuck here several more hours, which wouldn't be fair. As Carmen got off at seven, once again he'd have to ask her to watch Patrick. Theirs wasn't a perfect situation, but they'd been working things out just fine and, more importantly, Patrick seemed to like living with him.

Gavin smiled and waved back, thankful for Carmen for the tenth time that day. If she had a clue he actually appreciated her, she'd never let him live it down.

He nodded at Bethany as he headed to room three, thinking how pretty she was, while he maintained his professional physician demeanor. After he'd passed, he smiled and recalled what they'd done together that first night. And even though the focus of his life had changed since Patrick had moved in, he couldn't help but wonder if and how soon they could arrange to do it again. What would she think if she could read his mind?

Even an hour after the testing, a lingering itch drew his attention to his back. The meds had taken care of the worst of it, but a few areas still bothered him. He reached behind and, using his thumb, scratched the spot.

After examining the gastrointestinal bleeder and ordering a stat colonoscopy, opportunity knocked when the ER charge nurse walked by. But Bethany was nowhere in sight.

"Carmen? Can Patrick go home with you tonight? Looks like I'm needed around here."

"I told you, any time. Patrick and I are good buddies."

Maybe Patrick and Carmen were great friends, but it was obvious he missed his mother and was devastated by her sudden trip to England. And the big question was—could a man who'd been married to his job for the last three years be able to fill the gap?

He'd let both the boy and Maureen down during the marriage. Intent on establishing himself as a doctor, he'd left the majority of child-rearing on his wife's shoulders, though he had managed to have quality time with the boy whenever he'd been able to. She'd wanted to give up her career and be a stay-at-home mother, and he'd done his best to provide for them while still overwhelmed with medical school debts. He'd worked like a lunatic. And after the divorce Maureen had still wanted to stay at home…on Gavin's child support and alimony. He'd been accused of being a workaholic by more than a few people in his life, but he'd always felt it had been for a good cause.

For Patrick's sake, Gavin had promised to do everything in his power to make things right this time around, which meant thinking of his son first and, as tempting as she was, putting Bethany Caldwell completely out of his mind. Like that was going to happen.

* * *

Once things had settled down in the ER, and Beth had been officially discharged, she retreated from the pandemonium into the quiet hallway. She was tired. And hungry.

She went back to the allergy department to gather her belongings and head out to her car.

Dr Mehta would have to order a special RAST—radioallergosorbent—blood test for Gavin as she hadn't been able to finish reading the skin tests. And with his extreme reaction, it was important for him to know exactly what he was allergic to and what to avoid.

At least she now knew her mystery man's name and where he worked. Gavin had stirred feelings she'd never felt before, and if she was honest, she wanted to find out what else might happen with a man like him. Was that playing with fire? Yes. Was it dangerous? For her, yes. Would she actually allow herself to find out? Absolutely not. Until she knew the results of the pregnancy test, she'd do everything in her power to avoid him.

Beth started her car. The men in her life,

starting with her dad and ending with her ex-husband, had track records for being unreliable and undependable.

According to her best friend Jillian, who worked in the urgent care department, Gavin had more women throwing themselves at him than he could handle.

Of all the people to have had secret sex with.

Beth adjusted the rear-view mirror and shifted into reverse. Jillian always shared the scuttle-butt from ER and Dr Gavin Riordan could have any woman he wanted. So why would he be satisfied with just one? And in the world according to Beth, from now on she would settle for nothing less than being the only one.

She pulled the car out into the traffic and started her drive home, thinking about her failed marriage. Again. She'd always dreamed of having a big family. Her ex had never wanted kids, but hadn't mentioned it until after they'd had to get married. While her heart had broken more with each miscarriage, he'd seemed relieved. And she'd foolishly assumed her ex would be faithful. Wrong! She hadn't been able to trust him.

The fact that he'd been unable to satisfy her in bed over their two-year marriage might have had something to do with it. But Beth had never been good at faking anything, and she hadn't hidden that one important fact from him. Evidently his ego had only waited so long before he'd gone searching for a more responsive partner.

So long and good riddance.

If she was frigid, what could she call what had happened with Gavin that night? He'd taken her on a rocket trip to bliss in record time.

And now her period was late.

Was that her reward for finally cutting loose?

Damn.

If she did wind up being pregnant and she didn't miscarry, she'd keep the baby and figure out what to do about Gavin later.

The moment Beth opened the doors to the allergy department on Wednesday morning the phone rang. She swooped up the receiver, assuming it was the supervisor from the ER to tell her her fate.

"Allergy, this is Beth."

"You owe me dinner."

She heard Gavin's deep voice, loud and clear. Her heart rushed a beat or two.

"Are you there?" he asked when she paused.

"May I ask who's calling?" Lame!

After a brief hesitation he said, "It's Stud Muffin."

Her cheeks flamed faster than a brush fire. Obviously his son being present had kept him from saying what had been on his mind yesterday.

She stifled a giggle.

"I'll pick you up in front of the hospital on Friday night at seven…Sweet Cakes," he said.

How could she not smile? The guy was being silly and going overboard, trying to get her to laugh.

She played with a pen she'd picked up from the counter. Two could play this game. "I'm afraid 'Sweet Cakes' isn't available on Friday night. She works at the teen clinic in Venice." The pen shook in her hand.

"How late?"

She clicked the pen several times and heard an impatient sigh on the other end. She'd taken it too far. It also occurred to her that the poor man might have been up all night working—if the overflowing ER when she'd left last night had been any indication. Did he deserve her giving him a hard time? "I work until ten. You might be awfully hungry by then. I suggest we take a rain-check."

"Then let's have a drink and get to know each other. You can buy me dinner another night. I know where that clinic is—I'll pick you up from there on Friday."

She faltered. Had he just finagled two dates out of her? What about her plan to avoid him?

He sighed again. "Just say yes, Bethany. I need to get some sleep."

"Yes, Bethany, I need to get some sleep," she parroted softly, her mind swirling with what-ifs.

"Have a good day…Sweet Cakes." She heard a smile in his voice.

Would it be a good day after the lab called?

"Wait!" she said.

"Yes?"

"How's that boy, Andrew?"

Gavin cleared his throat. "The surgery went well. We'll have to wait and see if the hand will be functional. By the way, what you did with his sister was commendable. And my son. Thanks for that. I'll see you Friday."

She'd agreed to get-to-know-each-other drinks with a man she'd already had sex with. Well, what would "Stud Muffin" think about her predicament? He might change his dating tune if a certain lab test came back you-know-what. And more importantly, if she *was* pregnant, would she have the guts to tell him?

No sooner had she hung up than the phone rang again. On automatic reflex she gave the department name, followed by her own.

"This is Rick from the ER. I'm not sure if this is good news or not…but it's definitely news."

For the second time in two days Beth felt faint. "I'm pregnant?"

"Most definitely."

She couldn't remember afterwards if she'd said

thank you and goodbye or had just hung up, but suddenly she was standing in the allergy clinic with her arms tightly folded across her stomach to keep from falling apart. Her eyes stung. Nervous tingles made her skin prickle. Tears brimmed. She bit her lip to keep from crying out.

Maybe this third time the pregnancy would stick. Could she afford to be hopeful, again? Or should she be horrified? *I'm not married and I got knocked up on a one-night stand with a stranger.*

She'd always wanted children, but only under the right circumstances, in a loving relationship and preferably married. Talk about bad timing. Hell, she'd worked at the teen clinic long enough to know life threw everyone curve balls, but in this case she'd been the accomplice who'd helped the pitcher wind up and let fly.

And now, oh, God, she was pregnant.

On Thursday afternoon Gavin pushed through the swing doors into the allergy waiting room. At the nursing podium, Beth was in the middle of giving shots to one of her regular weekly patients. She'd just finished drawing up antigen from a vial when she spotted him.

Thanks to morning sickness, which seemed to be lasting all day, she didn't need any help with the sudden urge to vomit. Seeing him made her lose control and she dropped the vial. Damn. What could she do but try her best to act naturally? She felt out of control, as though someone had taken a hand mixer to her stomach.

She was pregnant and he was the father and somehow, some way, she'd have to tell him. But not now!

He nodded at her. "I need to set up an appointment for Patrick for asthma training."

"Sure." She managed to find her voice, nodding to the patient waiting for a shot and trying her hardest not to let the trembling of her hands show.

Navy blue slacks, pale blue shirt, colorful yellow tie, obviously just out of the shower with his hair still damp…he dripped confidence. And his woodsy scent had her thinking about being skin to skin with him and places she'd never been before. And though the smell soothed her queasy stomach, the memories whipped it right back up again.

Her patient cleared her throat. Right. The shot.

"I've been summoned," he said, pointing down the hall and continuing on toward Dr Mehta's office.

A few minutes later, just when Beth had calmed herself down, Gavin's voice startled her when he snuck up from behind.

He tossed some paperwork onto the podium. "I'm signing up for immunotherapy. Bupinder talked me into it."

Avoiding his eyes, she pretended to be engrossed with the doctor's orders. "Is that so?"

He leaned his forearm on the stand. "Guess I'll be one of your patients."

How could she face him every week of her pregnancy—that was, if she didn't miscarry this time? "I never read your test—how does she know what you're allergic to?"

"RAST test." A blood test where, if there was an allergy, the specific antibodies attached to a radioactive chemical. "You're right, I should be a bubble boy, but that's just me. I don't do anything halfway."

Recalling their crazy first encounter, she fought a blush. No. He definitely didn't do anything halfway.

She glanced up and saw a knowing smile, then quickly concentrated on her folded hands on the podium. She couldn't fall any deeper for his charm, not until he knew the facts and she knew where they stood.

"Be sure to pick up an EpiPen from the pharmacy and carry it with you at all times. We can't treat you for food allergies, just the pollens, so you've got to be prepared for another systemic reaction if it ever occurs."

She worked up the courage to make eye contact again. The tantalizing taupe stare forced a burst of nerves in her chest, and she caught her breath. She couldn't go on like this, and changed the subject. "When is a good time for the asthma training for Patrick?"

He looked into her eyes and smiled. "Any evening. You can come over to my place."

"Sorry, I don't do house calls."

"Not even for me?"

She sent him a pleading, exasperated glance—there were patients within earshot. He got the message. "What if I bring him in one afternoon next week?"

"Sure. Just bring him to the clinic. I'll make time for him." Putty in his hands.

"Sounds good. So is that all you need to talk to me about?"

Beth shot him a startled look. Why had he asked that? Did he know? Her mouth went dry. "After a systemic reaction like you had, we insist that you wait two weeks before starting the immunotherapy program. And don't forget to pick up your EpiPen."

"Sure thing." He slanted her a smile. "I'll see you tomorrow night."

He pushed himself off from the podium and strode toward the lobby, pushed through the swinging doors like a cowboy in a saloon, and left. She shamelessly checked out his behind. What got into her whenever he was around?

Dread trickled down her spine and quickly replaced the attraction to him. She'd have to tell Gavin sooner or later, and as they had a date tomorrow night, "sooner" *seemed* to be the best option.

But sooner stunk.

CHAPTER THREE

ON FRIDAY night at ten, Gavin drove his car to the front of the Venice Beach Teen clinic and parked. An old school chum of Patrick's had invited him to spend the weekend in Irvine, so Gavin was free. He needed a diversion from his inhumanly busy schedule and, having the night to himself, he looked forward to spending it with Bethany.

When he'd spotted her at the party last month, vibrant and appealing, he'd felt oddly energized by her spirit. This sweet young thing didn't deserve his usual post-divorce routine of hard work, easy loving, then saying goodbye. Now, with Patrick living with him, those days were officially over. He'd changed for his son's sake, and he didn't need a woman complicating things between the two of them. So why was he parked outside of a clinic in a bad part of town, looking forward to taking her for a drink?

Maybe because something more than sex had passed between Bethany and himself. It had started with a shock of a kiss that had reached inside and grabbed him. The electricity had been so fierce that he'd considered checking to make sure they hadn't been standing in water. Later, short-circuit sparks had turned into an all-out fire when they'd had sex. The way she'd surrendered to his touch, made him realize how special they had been together. It wasn't everyday you found someone as responsive as that. Tonight he hoped to get to know her to find out if his hunch was right—that she was a woman a man could fall for.

He gave an ironic laugh. Wasn't it just like life to dump the first woman in ages he'd really been intrigued by into his lap after he'd promised to be the father Patrick had never had but always deserved? And if he and Bethany did click tonight, how was he supposed to handle dating *and* Patrick?

He sat in the darkness of his car and watched

a group of five young adults leave the clinic in a straggly line. Their clothes ran the gamut from black, gauzy gothic to pullover preppy sweater to the new retro 1980s rock-star hairstyle, wrinkled T-shirts and skin-tight jeans. What was little Miss Florence Nightingale up to? And why did he find her so damn intriguing?

He hopped out of the car and crossed the street to meet her in the lobby. Her slim figure appeared in the foyer just as he reached the front door of the clinic. The bright fluorescent glow threw a halo around her soft honey-colored hair. He let out an amused chuckle at the image. She'd acted anything but angelic the night they'd met.

Instead of smiling when he approached, her eyes widened and she took a deep breath before she locked up the office. She didn't exactly look happy to see him.

Beth was the first to speak. "Feel like taking a walk? It's probably beautiful at the beach tonight."

"What happened to 'Hi, honey, I'm home. How was your day?'"

She gave him the requisite brief laugh for his

sorry attempt at humor, but she still looked anxious. And it was beginning to rub off on him.

On impulse, he tugged her close and pecked her on the cheek. "Hi, honey, I'm home." He inhaled her scent, peaches and vanilla, good enough to eat, then led her out the front door. "Would you rather take a walk than have a drink?"

"Well…" Looking flustered from the kiss, she brushed hair away from her face. "We could stop at the corner store and buy a couple of sodas and do both."

They crossed the street. He opened the door and held it for her as she slid into the passenger seat. "I don't want to accuse you of being cheap, but you're easy on the pocketbook, Bethany. Not that I'm complaining." He circled the car and got inside.

"It's been a stressful week. I'm just thinking I could use a walk, if you don't mind." So far she'd managed to evade making eye contact with him.

"Whatever the lady wants. The sea breeze might do me some good, too." He started the engine, liking the idea of a sultry beach walk with Bethany. Maybe it would help her shake those tense vibes she was giving off.

He pulled out from the curb into the boulevard bustle. Headlights from oncoming traffic illuminated the interior of the car and he glimpsed her expressive almond-shaped eyes watching him. She definitely looked anxious and quickly looked away. As she hadn't said another thing, he'd start things off with small talk. "So, what do you do at the clinic?"

She cleared her throat. "Two nights a week, I'm an STD counselor for teenagers."

He sputtered a laugh. Just his luck, she was a sexually transmitted disease counselor, and she'd probably preach about it non-stop. "A safe sex crusader, are you?"

"I do my best."

"Does anyone listen?"

"Sometimes."

"Is that enough?" Hmm. She'd probably just come from the clinic that Friday night last month, too. They'd used protection, and she'd been the one to produce it.

"Enough? It has to be. They sure don't pay me much." She smiled. "This counseling job comes with small rewards, not huge successes." She tossed him a brief, resigned glance and returned to looking out of the passenger window.

Had he done something wrong? He liked the way things had started out between them at the party. Though he hadn't exactly been a gentleman where Bethany was concerned, tonight he'd planned to begin making up for it, if she'd give him a chance.

Silence filled the car until he thought he would suffocate. Not a great way to start. Gavin opened the window and hung his elbow outside, letting a fresh rush of air in. It was probably time to acknowledge the giant elephant between them in the car. They'd had sex. Great sex.

"Good thing I wore protection that night."

She barely gave him a chance to finish his sentence. "You have to understand, what we did was crazy and totally unlike me."

He gave her a wry smile. "I liked you just fine. And for the record, that was way out of character for me, too." He tried to keep his eyes on the road, but sensed something was terribly wrong with his date.

She made a pitiful attempt at a smile.

OK. She felt guilty.

Was there something she wasn't telling him?

The hair on his neck prickled.

Gavin drank cola and walked at arm's length from Bethany along the damp shoreline sand. The night was brisk with a pungent algae scent, typical of the Pacific Ocean in April. Beth had loosened up a bit, though their conversation after the hot topic had reverted to being superficial and safe.

Gavin gazed at the sky, a vast, thick blanket of black with thousands of pinprick stars. He threw a seashell at it, as if trying to make contact with the heavens.

"If you ruled the world, Bethany..." His voice tore at the silence between them. "What would be different?"

She stopped in her tracks, took a long draw on her soda, and thought for a moment. "Teenagers would think twice before jumping between the sheets with the first hot guy or girl they met, and I'd practice what I preach."

OK, so she'd just come from work, and loud and clear he'd gotten the message. Gavin finished his drink and crushed the can.

What had happened to the Bethany Caldwell he'd met last month? She hadn't been kidding when she'd said it had been a fluke. Suddenly Gavin needed a real drink. He'd have to work extra hard if he wanted a second chance with Bethany. "Listen, there's a beach bar up the way. What do you say to a couple of daiquiris?" He flashed his most persuasive grin.

"Actually, I've sworn off daiquiris, and all alcohol in general."

A cold breeze picked up from the shore. So she wasn't about to make herself vulnerable again. He could live with that. He really didn't have time for dating anyway. He'd take her back to her car and kiss her goodbye, for good.

"But I could use a nice cup of herbal tea."

And he could use a beer.

After the herbal tea comment, she gave him a smile so fine he almost tripped in the sand. What was he supposed to do with a woman who managed to steal his composure and change his plans with just one look?

An hour and one cup of tea later, Beth sat gazing into the deep-brown eyes of one rugged and frustratingly appealing man. He'd pulled out all stops, insisting on charming her out of her foul mood. She rested her chin in the palm of her hand and flirted with a man who not only excited and frightened her but who'd managed to knock her up on the first try. How the hell was she supposed to tell him?

"Patrick and I are getting to know each other all over again. I have to kick myself for not being there more for him when he was younger. I was always so distracted with work. I guess I left a lot up to his mother."

She nodded, happily amazed he'd give her such personal information so soon.

"At first I was angry when Maureen took off and left him with me. Sounds selfish, huh?"

"Maybe a little."

"She insisted on full custody when we divorced. I fought like hell against it, but I didn't have enough confidence to think I could handle a six-year-old on my own. Now, after three years, she suddenly changes her mind and takes off for Oxford, not caring how disruptive it is to Patrick and me."

Speaking of disrupted lives, could her pregnancy timing be any worse? Just when the man was renewing his relationship with his son, she'd have to drop a pregnancy bomb on him. It was painfully clear how much Patrick needed him now. But if she didn't miscarry, wouldn't she need Gavin, too?

"Now," he said, "I think it's the best thing that could have ever happened. I love having him around."

"He's a great kid, and you seem like a good father."

His intense gaze softened. She liked the way the corners of his eyes crinkled when his smile stretched to a grin.

"Thanks for the vote of confidence." He put his

hand on hers. "For the record, Patrick thinks you're 'neat'."

"Neat?" she repeated, feeling warmly flattered. "You talked about me?"

"Oh, yeah. He thought it was 'totally cool' how you passed out." He gently stroked her thumb. "I think you're 'neat' too."

Every bit of his body language screamed, *Male*! She'd felt it firsthand five weeks ago when he'd taken her in his arms and kissed her stupid. From his salt and pepper brown hair to his straight, strong nose, to his broad shoulders and strong hands, the man oozed testosterone. She could practically smell it. Cutting herself some slack, she admitted she hadn't stood a chance of resisting him that night.

A waitress interrupted Beth's borderline gawking. "More tea?"

"Oh, no, thanks. Not for me."

Following her lead, Gavin gestured for the check. He quickly returned his attention to Beth, giving her a knowing look. She flushed under the heat of his stare.

Beth had never been more enraptured than that night with Gavin. In her heart she'd always known she wasn't the ice goddess her ex had insisted she was. It had just been a matter of finding the right man, and Gavin had undeniably discovered her secret flame. He'd rocked her world, opening up all kinds of new possibilities. It was about time she had the chance to enjoy a satisfying physical relationship with a man. With Gavin. But now she was pregnant. And he was grappling with being a single dad. Their timing couldn't have been worse.

The dim light dappled his masculine smile in deep creases, accentuating the cleft in his chin and making him all the more appealing.

She worried about how he might want to handle their "situation". But where the baby was concerned, she'd be in total control. A burst of panic clutched her stomach and sent it spinning. She gazed back into his enticing eyes and momentarily forgot what she'd been worrying about.

They sat awkwardly grinning at each other until the waitress brought the check. He paid then reached for her hand as they walked to the parking lot. She let him weave their fingers together. The feel of his palm against hers was exciting.

Gavin led her to the car and let go of her hand. A subtle unspoken promise from the bar became reality when he reached for her face. Skipping any more small talk, he kissed her, holding her close. Forgetting every promise she'd made about never kissing Gavin again until he knew, Beth welcomed him. She grew light-headed and weak at the knees with Gavin's fiery kiss and strong caresses. She anchored herself to his chest, arms locked around his neck. Blood rushed to her head.

He quickly progressed to hard, deeper kisses and she matched each one with surprising hunger. Gavin walked her backward and leaned his full weight into her, pressing her against the side of the car. His body felt solid and hot. She nuzzled his neck, savoring the feel of his skin as a musky masculine smell made her want to taste him. Everywhere.

The flow of traffic from the nearby boulevard

competed with the sound of the high tide across the road. She felt his heart pounding against her chest, amazed that she had caused such a riot. All those extraneous sounds faded away.

He kissed her again and she lost every thought.

Just once more. She'd be with him one more time then she'd tell him.

His hands dropped from her shoulders. He stepped back. Confusion and passion battled in his stare. "Look what you do to me. What am I going to do with you?"

Riding the sensual rush, she couldn't get her mouth to form a single word. He leaned beside her, rubbed her arm and looked deeply into her eyes as though ready to say something more.

His cellphone blared an annoying familiar jingle. Beth jumped. It rang again.

"Dr Riordan." He sounded as though he'd just run a mile. He listened for a few seconds and gave a deep sigh, then swallowed. "OK, I'll be there as soon as I can."

Gavin folded up the cellphone, backed away, and regretfully looked at Beth. "They need me.

Dr McGuire's wife went into premature labor." He scrubbed his face and stretched. "I've got to cover for him in the ER so he can be with her for the delivery. Hell, I don't even have time for a cold shower. They're short-handed as it is, and apparently the waiting room's bursting at the seams."

Beth remembered to breathe. The ER waiting room wasn't the only thing ready to burst at the seams. She attempted to recover her composure and fussed with her hair. She'd been saved from herself. The moment of passion had passed, signaled by a cool descending curtain of reality. Work. Responsibilities.

Pregnancy.

But he still deserved to know about her condition. A sudden rush of nerves made her fingers go into spasm as she pulled her sweater together and buttoned it. *Tell him now.*

After two miscarriages, something held her back. As much as it would pain her, maybe history would repeat itself, and she'd never have to let Gavin know.

"I guess you should drive me to my car, then."

"Bethany." Gavin placed his hand on hers to prevent her from getting any farther away. The touch burned.

Gavin brushed her lips again, slowly luring her back into a trance. He pressed his forehead to hers. "Have dinner with me tomorrow night?"

She hesitated. "I…I can't."

Gavin looked confused and in need of an explanation. "No" couldn't have been a word he was used to hearing. But this craziness had to stop. She couldn't keep seeing him, wanting him, without telling him. He was trouble, with all the trimmings. With her luck, she'd lose her head, and if she repeated her lifelong pattern, next she'd lose her heart, and once she told him about the pregnancy, she'd probably lose him altogether. She needed more time to think things through.

"I promised my mother I'd fill in for her at the Hollywood soup kitchen."

He smiled. "That's an excuse I've never heard before."

"It's true. She's been working there on Saturday nights for years, since my father died. I used to help out all the time until I took the teen clinic job. My mother's arthritis has been acting up—the least I can do is help her out tomorrow night."

He studied her with intelligent eyes and lifted a single doubtful brow. "Maybe I'll stop by. Patrick isn't coming home until Sunday afternoon." He opened the car door and helped her inside before she could protest. He closed the door and walked to the driver's side.

So Gavin Riordan was determined to see her again. An odd flutter of satisfaction confused her, but she still hadn't told him about the pregnancy. Things were bound to change once she did.

After a silent drive, Gavin delivered Beth back to the clinic and her car. He leaned across the seat and kissed her one last smoldering time, said goodbye and, once again, left her breathless and completely shaken.

Once safely inside her car, she watched him drive into the night toward the rolling sounds of the high tide as waves crashed onto the shore.

She'd skipped her chance to tell him her news. It had been on the tip of her tongue so many times. She knew she had to do it. The guy deserved to know. But her painful memories of losing two babies prevented her from having confidence this pregnancy would go to term. Wait. Wait a little longer.

Could things get any more complicated? He seemed like such a regular guy when he'd opened up. They definitely had chemistry, and it would be a shame not to get to know him better. But why bother when he wouldn't ever be able to give her what she'd wanted more than anything—marriage and a family of her own? He'd already had both.

It was clear he needed to give all of his attention to his son. Patrick deserved no less. But didn't he have the right to know about her baby? If she told him, it would change everything. And if she miscarried again, the damage to their new relationship would already be done. Maybe she shouldn't tell him just yet.

A sudden thought popped into her head. Her test was in the hospital computer. All he had to do was look her up.

What if he found out before she told him?

CHAPTER FOUR

AT THREE o'clock in the morning, Gavin stood before his fifteenth patient. He had already diagnosed a silent MI, admitted a patient with a colitis flare-up, summoned the police for suspected spousal abuse for another, tended to the survivor of a traffic accident, and delegated the broken bones and lacerations to his PA and newest resident.

He hadn't been the only extra person called in. Carmen had been, too, and he had been grateful for her presence over the past few hours. Divorced with an empty nest, she was always willing to go the extra mile for the ER. Now, with yet another case, he asked for Carmen's assistance with the procedure.

A seventy-six-year-old patient had been brought in with a huge abdomen. The chart indicated that the patient had been diagnosed with advanced prostate cancer three months ago, it had metastasized to his liver, and the decreased liver function had caused a build-up of fluid in his belly, known as ascites.

Gavin had seen the skeleton-thin man with a stomach the size of a watermelon hobble into the emergency room, assisted by his equally frail wife. The man was hardly able to breathe from the pressure of the ascites, and this procedure would be a quality-of-life issue instead of a cure. Gavin prepared to perform a paracentesis to remove the excess fluid from the patient's abdominal cavity to make him more comfortable.

"Did my nurse explain this procedure to you before you signed the consent, Mr Ingersoll?"

The stoic senior solemnly nodded his head. Gavin gingerly assisted the man onto his side near the edge of the gurney.

Carmen pushed a stainless-steel surgical stand with all of the needed equipment toward Gavin then placed several large evacuation jars on another table. She handed him a package of sterile gloves and seemed to read his mind, offering each sterilized item for his use before he had the chance to ask. They worked well together.

After numbing the area, Gavin inserted a needle into the patient's flesh, puncturing the skin and entering the abdominal cavity just enough to reach the fluid build-up. It drained through the tube, pink and frothy.

He looked at the man and smiled into dark sunken sockets where he suspected bright eyes had once dwelt. "We may need to drain several bottles from the look of your abdomen, Mr Ingersoll."

The old gentleman smiled back to confirm the painlessness of the procedure making the best of unpleasant circumstances. "Now I know how my wife felt all those years ago when she was pregnant with our kids. I used to tease her about waddling like a duck—guess it's come back to bite me in the ass. Now I'm the one with the wide load."

"I've always thought women look great when they're pregnant," Gavin said.

"To each his own. I take it you have kids?"

Gavin's bedside smile faded. "One." He wondered how Patrick was doing, spending the weekend at his friend's house. Even after a month of living together, Patrick seemed troubled and secretive and at times Gavin didn't have a clue how to reach out to him. He loved his son, but no one had taught him how to be a father in medical school. And if they had handed out grades in parenting, he'd have to repeat the course. But he wouldn't give up.

When Patrick had been a baby and toddler, Gavin had been a resident and had worked eighty-hour weeks, and though it had been the last thing he'd wanted, he'd hardly had time to spend with him. He'd missed Patrick's first words and steps, and heaven only knew how many other things. He shook his head at his loss.

Too bad they didn't offer do-overs for parents. But this time, while his ex-wife was away, he'd have a second chance. He didn't intend to fail again. "I have a son who's almost ten."

"Be sure to spend lots of time with him. Boys need their fathers at that age."

"Will do," he said, intending to do just that.

Clamping the tubing off, he made a switch from one full bottle to another empty one, the third. He palpated Mr Ingersoll's abdomen, which was growing softer and flabbier by the minute. Gavin glanced at the monitor above the bed. Sure enough, the patient's oxygen saturation reading was coming up nicely. By the end of the procedure, he would no longer need supplementary oxygen.

After Carmen had marked the latest vital signs on the patient chart, she helped finish the procedure by applying a pressure dressing to the patient's tiny abdominal puncture wound. He'd leave the rest up to her.

Gavin wrote up notes stuck inside a makeshift clipboard. Up until now, he hadn't had a spare moment to think about Beth and the crazy things she did to his libido and good sense. But now he let his mind drift to the woman who could make him howl at the moon by merely fluttering her thick brown lashes. He smiled and relaxed a tiny bit then quickly tensed.

What horrible timing. Bethany was a complication he didn't need right now, but he couldn't convince himself to forget her.

Patrick even liked her, which was a good sign. She and his son seemed to have great rapport, which would be important with any woman he wanted to date at this point in his life. But he didn't want to date just any woman—he wanted to date Beth.

First he'd have to convince her to let down her guard. Something seemed to be bothering her. She'd been so tense and skittish when he'd first picked her up tonight, and he'd had to work extra hard to make her smile. But he'd finally broken through at the bar and later in the parking lot, where he'd thoroughly enjoyed the payoff, a goodnight kiss that practically set his socks on fire.

His pleasant thoughts were interrupted when

Carmen rushed up to him. "Call for you. Patrick's having another asthma attack."

At ten a.m. on Saturday morning, Beth sat in her favorite spot in the tiny, one-bedroom apartment she called home. She preferred to call it quaint and cozy as this was all she could afford. The sun brightened the kitchen nook where she lounged, warming her face and spirit. It was a new day, and there was no sign of morning sickness—though the idea of being pregnant still stunned her.

Having completed her weekly check-in call to her mother, avoiding her "big news" by peppering her with small talk and arranging their monthly lunch date with her the next day, she dialed her friend Jillian.

Beth's gray tabby, Lila, stretched to twice her normal length along the breakfast nook bench beside her. She pushed at Beth's thigh with small pink paws and let out a little sound, leaving the tip of her tongue showing between her tiny front teeth. And though Beth didn't have a whole lot to smile about today, she grinned and tickled the cat's ears, chin, and belly until Jillian picked up on the fourth ring.

Caller ID had her friend jumping right in. "So what happened with the doc? Tell me."

Beth smiled and lifted her coffee-mug for another sip of decaf, fully aware that Jillian wanted to hear all the dirty details of her date.

"Come on, spill. I couldn't sleep I was so excited for you. What's he like?"

"He's actually very nice." Beth combed her fingers through her hair. "Charming, in fact."

"I've heard he's incredible."

Beth covered her eyes, squinting. "In what way? Does he sleep around a lot? Just how many nurses know how 'incredible' he is?"

"Now, don't get all excited, it's not like that. You know, a friend of a friend of a nurse who dated him a few times a long time ago. That's all. He's just so sexy and, you know, a *real* man. Every woman in Urgent Care is curious what he'd be like."

It wasn't morning sickness, but Beth's stomach flip-flopped. What had she been thinking? He had his son to take care of and the busiest ER in a fifty-mile radius to run. But under the circumstances, whether she liked it or not, she was bound to have a relationship with Gavin for the baby's sake.

"Well, I'm not going to be your 'source' for gossip where Gavin Riordan is concerned. Don't even think about repeating what I'm about to tell you."

"I swear! You know I wouldn't."

"The truth is, he sweeps me off my feet and I find myself doing things I wouldn't normally do and I don't want to get…well…hurt."

"Did you have sex again?"

"No!"

"Why can't you just think of it as an adventure? Put a spin on it. Take him to bed again, enjoy yourself, then *you* be the one to dump *him*."

Beth made an exasperated face. "Does that sound remotely like anything I would ever do, Jillian?" If only the problem was as simple as deciding to have sex with Gavin again.

"You did sleep with him before you knew who he was."

Beth sighed. "Don't remind me." She glanced down at her stomach—the part of her body that would betray her circumstances soon enough—and prayed for more grace time. "Do not breathe a word of what I'm about to say to anyone, or I'll cut off your thumbs. I swear I will." Lila jumped off her lap and ran down the hall.

"What? You know you can trust me. I only repeat other people's gossip back to you. Not the other way around."

Gossip. Oh, Lord. It would be inevitable.

"Right." Beth shook her head and glanced toward the ceiling. Deep down, she knew she could trust Jillian with her secret, but something held her back.

Dead silence.

"Hello? Has our connection been cut?" Jillian asked impatiently.

"No." Bethany finally found a word. Gavin deserved to know before she told anyone else, even her best friend. "He's a fantastic kisser. The best I've ever known."

"I knew it."

"There's one other thing." Bethany turned her coffee-mug round and round on the table. "Listen, I just found out on Wednesday…I need to fill in for my mother at the soup kitchen tonight. They're always short-staffed, and I desperately need your help."

Later that afternoon, the institution-sized drably painted church kitchen on the corner of Highland and Franklin Avenue hummed with half a dozen people. Beth was thankful for the distraction. It had been a few months since she'd helped out, and had to follow one of the regulars around to get re-oriented. The helpers knew her mother, and how hard she had worked for the cause all these years in the soup kitchen, and treated Beth respectfully. Feeling a twinge of guilt, Beth wished she hadn't drifted away over the last year.

Jillian stood on a stool and poured super-sized can after can of cut green beans into an enormous pot on the stove. Beth worried she'd fall or, worse, burn herself on the extra-large oven. The seasoned volunteer handed Beth three big bags of frozen chicken pieces. "Here. All you've got to do is lay them out on the pans and bake them for thirty minutes. They're pre-seasoned."

She glanced at the extra-large, multi-layered oven gratefully. Beth turned and almost bumped into another volunteer. Man, the place was crawling with bodies. She put on an apron to trick herself into thinking she knew what she was doing. At least it wasn't complicated.

A half-hour later the loyal crew of white-haired church regulars busied themselves with cleaning tables and putting folding chairs in place in the dining hall. Corn bread was stacked up on the counters. The steam table was turned on and ready to keep the food hot until it was served.

"OK, everybody, ten minutes and we're ready to roll," the lead volunteer called out.

A loud rapping on the back door snapped Beth out of her thoughts. She glanced at Jillian, who shrugged her shoulders and strode over to find out who it was. Jillian swung the door open and Beth saw Gavin standing outside, holding a huge box of assorted fresh fruit. Patrick stood beside him, struggling with a filled-to-the-brim paper bag.

Beth rushed to the door as Jillian stood looking stunned with a wide-eyed stare and open mouth.

"Dr Riordan?" Jillian finally asked.

"May we come in? These are heavy."

"Of course." Beth reached for Patrick's bag, trying her best to act nonchalant. "Hey, hi Patrick." She'd focus on the boy and hope his dad would disappear, though she'd already noticed he'd arrived in casual tight denims and a slim-fitting T-shirt. Maybe she could rethink that promise to herself about telling Gavin she was pregnant the very next time she saw him, and postpone it until after the next time they'd kissed?

"I've brought enough fruit to feed a crowd. Will this be enough?"

"More than enough."

He carefully placed the box on the closest countertop and turned back toward Beth, folding his arms in a take-charge manner. "I know a guy at the Gold Coast farmers' market. I thought your guests might enjoy it. I can arrange for him to supply fresh fruit and veggies every week, if you'd like. Just say the word."

"I can't believe you." Impressed with the gesture, she couldn't take her eyes off him. Distracted by his sexy appearance, she liked what she saw. If only things could be different. "I'm going to have Clarence, the lead volunteer, hold you to that offer."

"No problem." Gavin shot her a knowing grin. "I'm for real, sweetheart." He leaned in closer. "Or should I say Sweet Cakes?" His teasing brown eyes almost made her drool. Instead, she cuffed him on the arm, rolled her eyes, and acted insulted.

Twenty minutes later, joy beamed from several diners' faces as they savored, along with the beans, baked chicken and cornbread, assorted apples, nectarines, bananas and grapes, compliments of Gavin Riordan, M.D.

Beth stood in the kitchen, gazing out into the dining hall, enjoying what she saw, though dreading the conversation to come.

One thing was for sure, the man caused excitement in her veins and a quickening of her heartbeat every time she saw him, and she didn't seem to have any control over it. She'd love a chance to know him for who he was instead of having to find out how he'd react to her news. But it would be the true test of his character. All things considered, she'd still rather get to know him in a more traditional manner, like dating, rather than sharing parenthood.

Gavin looked especially tired today when he approached with a plate of food in each hand. "How about having dinner with me? I've reserved two seats in a cozy little corner right next to the biker with the bushy gray beard, the skinhead and the little old lady who seems to be having a conversation with my son." He lifted his brows and made nice with his delicious brown eyes.

Beth wanted to purr like Lila.

He handed her a plate, nudged her lower back and said, "After we eat, I thought I'd set up an impromptu blood-pressure clinic here. You can help."

Beth found out Gavin had pulled an overnighter at Mercy's ER and had got an emergency call that Patrick had had another asthma flare-up. He'd driven down to Irvine, where Patrick had spent the night with his friend, administered a breathing treatment and brought his son home early that morning.

After such a tough night and long day, why would he bother to come here?

After dinner, Gavin brought in his doctor's bag, complete with portable blood-pressure monitor, and while Beth took vital signs for the diners, he did a quick head and neck exam on anyone who wanted it. In between patients, they chatted.

"What made you come here today?" she asked.

"I tried to take a nap this afternoon." He palpated the neck of an elderly man, then felt his thyroid. "And suddenly your face came to me. I thought it was an omen or something." He flashed his penlight up the man's nostrils, then asked him to say "Ah" and looked down his throat.

She shook her head while studying him. He looked tired, with dark circles under his eyes, but still managed to be devastatingly handsome.

"Mr Stanley, I want you to come to the Mercy Hospital ER tomorrow. Your lymph nodes are swollen and you need more tests."

"I don't have health insurance," the man said.

"You come to the ER and we'll take care of you. Here." He fished out his business card. "Tell them Dr Riordan sent you."

The man agreed, took Gavin's card and left.

In between patients, Beth said, "That omen stuff was such a crock."

He grinned. "Very perceptive. Here's the deal." Gavin peeled off his disposable gloves and donned another pair preparing for the next patient. "I need you to teach Patrick about his asthma. I thought if I bribed you by bringing a boatload of fruit, you might come home with us and do your spiel."

"Wow." Beth focused in on the elevated blood pressure of a young pregnant woman. "Are you under a doctor's care, Gina?"

"I went to the free clinic when I first got pregnant."

"Gavin, can you check this out?"

Beth switched arms and rechecked the blood pressure reading. It was still elevated.

"Are you watching your salt intake?" Beth asked.

The woman shrugged.

"Are you eating a lot of fast food?"

"It's cheap, and I'm hungry a lot."

"It's cheaper to buy fresh food and cook it yourself," Beth said.

"I don't have a kitchen where I stay. Besides, I don't know how to cook."

Fighting off a wave of depression, all Beth could think to do was pat the young woman's hand and smile empathetically at her. Gavin pressed on her ankles and noticed she had pitting edema. "How long have your feet and ankles been this way?"

"What way?"

"Swollen."

"I dunno."

"Your blood pressure is borderline, and you need to find out if your blood sugar is elevated. Are you diabetic?"

"Dia—what?"

"Gina, what do you think about paying a visit to the free clinic's urgent care tonight?" Gavin asked.

"I don't have any way of getting there."

One of the gray-haired volunteers, who'd been intently following the progress, spoke up. "I'll be glad to drive you."

Gavin nodded to the young woman. "I think it's a good idea that you go. You might need to be on blood-pressure medicine, and the doctors need to check out the progress of your baby. What do you say?"

"Can I finish my dinner first?"

Gavin gave a benevolent smile. "Of course." He turned to the volunteer. "That's very kind of you to offer to drive her. Thank you."

"That's what we're here for, isn't it? To help each other out."

"You're right about that."

"Hey, Doc, any chance you could do this once a month?"

Gavin glanced around at the makeshift clinic, an idea flashing in his eyes. "You know, I can probably get some of the first-year med students who need community service over here every month. I'll get back to you on that." He handed out another business card and they shook hands.

Seeing no one else in line, Gavin packed up his bag. Beth replaced the BP monitor in its case. Touched by his willingness to examine several of the homeless and downtrodden and arrange for future clinics, she had a change of heart about his earlier offer.

"You know I want to help Patrick, but do you need me tonight?"

"I wouldn't ask if I wasn't really concerned. His attacks seem to be getting worse and closer together. I know how to treat them, but I want him to learn how to take control. You know, to empower him over his condition."

How could she refuse? The boy needed to get his asthma regulated. Dread drilled a hole in the pit of her stomach at the thought of being alone with Gavin at his house. "I've got to help with cleanup." She gestured toward the cluttered dining hall and kitchen, still hoping for a way out and anxious to break away.

Gavin shot out of his chair. "I'll help."

"Oh, no. You've done enough already and, besides, you've been up all night. I couldn't possibly let you do that." Beth scanned the white-haired crew.

"Just tell me what to do," he said.

She asked the leader, a frail, hunched-over, seventy-ish man, what they both could do.

"Well, you can sweep the floors."

Gavin looked surprised.

The old guy shoved a broom in Gavin's hand. "After that you can mop."

Beth gave Gavin a surprised, apologetic smile.

He grinned back at her. "I happen to be very skilled at mopping floors. I worked as a janitor one semester during college." He looked back at the old man. "Have they got the big rolling bucket with the mop wringer thingy here?"

"Of course. You're a real inspiration, Doc. Follow me." The man stopped and looked at Beth. "You go help wash the dishes."

She set Patrick up with the fun water spray detail and had him rinse off all the dishes before she stacked them into the institution-style dish-washer, the way she'd been shown.

An hour later, all the volunteers had left except the leader, and cleanup was almost finished. Beth was trying to find the pantry door key when she heard Jillian's cackle. She peered round the corner to see what was going on. Jillian, with her wild mane of red curls, stood with her arm around Patrick's narrow shoulders, spying through the kitchen door. Beth walked up behind them and looked into the dining hall.

The floor had been mopped and looked spotless. In the corner sat Gavin on two folding chairs, one for his feet and one for his behind, with his head hung over the back, slack jawed and sound asleep. He'd mopped himself into the corner and must have decided to wait while the floor dried. The sight was endearingly funny. Beth fought a crazy urge to kiss him awake.

"Patrick," she said. "Go wake your father. It's time to leave."

The boy did so. "Dad!" Not at all what she'd had in mind for waking up the poor man.

Gavin sat straight up, snapping back into consciousness. "What?" He wiped his face with both hands, grimaced and tried to focus on where he was. Patrick giggled.

Gavin squinted and looked beyond his son to concentrate on Beth's face. "I'm fine."

She walked across the room. "Here's the plan," she said before he could say another word. "I'll drop Jillian off at home, go get my patient education bag and meet you at your house."

"But I want dessert," Patrick said.

"No problem. I'll bring some cookies with me."

"Yay. Peanut-butter cookies. OK?"

"Sure." She glanced back at Gavin, who was still shaking the sleep from his head. "You gonna be OK?"

"Absolutely." Gavin stretched and yawned. He staggered on his way to standing, as though his foot had gone to sleep, and attempted a good-natured smile.

"Follow me." She draped her arm around Patrick's shoulder and led him toward the door. Gavin and Jillian followed a few feet behind.

When they reached his Mercedes, Jillian said, "Holy hot tuna, Dr Riordan, they sure pay you well at Mercy Hospital."

Gavin looked at Beth. "Hardly well enough according to my ex-wife." He gave Beth directions to his house, glanced at his watch and clapped his hands together. "OK, so how soon should I have some coffee ready?"

An hour later, Beth drove on streets she rarely had reason to. Upscale and exclusive, the area where Gavin had directed her seemed of another world despite being only a few minutes from her apartment. She proceeded up a winding, narrow road and pulled the car up in front of what looked like a mansion.

A huge California Spanish-style villa complete with an arched porch and massive decorative wrought-iron fencing rose before her. In awe, she shut her mouth. She agreed with Jillian, they must pay him well at Mercy Hospital.

He'd been waiting and the wrought-iron gates

opened for her to enter. Once she had parked and walked up the steps, he greeted her again.

Inside, Beth tried her best not to gawk. Real artwork adorned the warm brick-red walls; soft leather chairs and couches, sconces, chandeliers and sculptures filled the rooms, each with its own fireplace. She felt out of place amidst such wealth.

Gavin approached her with the same look on his face as the night before when he'd walked her to the car. Wasn't he tired? And where was Patrick?

Beth struggled to breathe. Why did he torment her so? Her mouth felt dry, but she needed to tell him.

"Let me get your sweater." He touched her neck when he helped take it off. Chills tickled on her skin and she tried her best to ignore what he did to her ear.

He caught her mouth with a soft kiss that robbed her of breath. She wanted to kiss him back, but that wasn't why she'd come. She longed for more of his sweet talk and crafty moves but tonight, after she was through with

Patrick, she had to tell him the truth and face the consequences.

She dared to look Gavin in the face and found dark, smoldering eyes drawing her deeper under his spell. She tore away in time to find Patrick entering the room.

"This place is spectacular," she blurted.

"Thanks," Gavin replied, watching her. "It was a gift from my grandmother."

"She left it to Dad in her will," Patrick added, sounding like an expert on wills and probate.

"I see."

"I grew up here," Gavin offered with eyes filled with memories. "My parents split up, and my grandmother raised me. When I got married, and she was ready to move into senior housing, she insisted we move in. With the outrageous cost of realty in California, it was an offer I couldn't refuse."

Beth nodded at Gavin's good fortune, and Patrick took her hand. "You want to see my room?"

An hour later, she and Patrick giggled in the living room when she had him demonstrate how to use the peak-flow meter again. He'd taken in a deep breath, put his mouth on the device then made the mistake of looking at Beth. For some reason, for the third time in a row, he must have felt silly and laughed, and Beth giggled along with him. It had been a long evening. He showed signs of being giddy, looking tired and rubbing his eyes.

"OK. So you understand how to record your peak-flow readings on this sheet, right?"

"Yes." He yawned and smiled, making a silly face.

She tried not to laugh, again. He really was a cute kid. "And you know how to take both of your inhalers?"

He nodded.

"Which one is your rescue inhaler?"

He pointed to the gray canister.

"Do you use it every day?"

He shook his head, wispy light-brown hair flopping around.

How could she hold his attention for the next few minutes? Gavin was sprawled out on the sofa, looking sleepy, but she guessed he'd listened to every word she'd said. He was merely trying to be inconspicuous while he monitored how well Patrick followed the lesson on asthma care.

"One more question before you get that cookie. As I recall, you were allergic to grass and some trees. Do you remember if your cat test got itchy and bumpy?" She noticed a tiny response in his eyes. They got bigger momentarily then he quickly looked away. "Does your friend, by any chance, have a cat?"

"No," he quickly responded. "Can I go now?"

Beth knew when she'd worn out her educator welcome. "OK, but remember to stay away from your asthma triggers. When you've finished playing outside, put your dirty clothes in the hamper right away. And always shower at night so you won't get the pollen in your hair all over your pillow. And if something makes you wheeze, remember what it is and avoid it."

He'd already made it halfway to the kitchen before she finished the sentence. She glanced at Gavin, whose eyes had popped open.

"I think he'll need another session with you.

Want to stick around for the night so you can pick up where you left off tomorrow morning?"

Knowing he wasn't serious, she rolled her eyes. "As if." All kidding aside, she knew now was the time to tell him. She couldn't put it off another second. She took a deep breath. "Listen, Gavin?"

He sat up with a playful, sexy glaze in his eyes. "Yes?"

"Will you stop for a moment, please? I've got something important to tell you."

He took her seriously and immediately changed his demeanor. "OK."

Oh God, how should she say it? She'd practiced non-stop on the drive over, and had thought she had the perfect words, but now her mind went totally blank. How hard was it to say, "I'm pregnant"? She sighed, and distracted herself by cleaning up her asthma education equipment and charts.

A strong, warm hand wrapped around her wrist and stopped her. She looked into his inquisitive eyes and swallowed.

"What do you need to tell me?"

She blew a light breath through her lips and

tried to ignore the butterflies in her stomach. He didn't let go. "Well, it's been exactly five weeks since we…ah…met."

"I remember it well. Go on."

"And earlier this week when I passed out, they ran some lab tests on me."

His grasp grew the slightest bit tighter. He stared intently into her eyes. She blinked. "How should I put this?"

His head tilted the tiniest bit and his eyes grew more serious.

"The thing is…I'm pregnant," she whispered.

Instead of a huge reaction, he didn't move. His hand stayed exactly where it had been with the same amount of pressure, his head tilted in the same direction. The only thing different about his expression was a raised brow. "You're pregnant," he repeated, as if he hadn't heard her correctly.

"That's right." She nodded, suddenly thankful the horrible moment of truth was over. Now all she had to do was live with the fallout, and from the look of Gavin, he was neither shocked nor pleased.

"And do you have any plans for this pregnancy?"

She sucked in a quick breath. "I…I plan to keep the baby."

In that instant, Patrick appeared at the door. "Dad? Will you put me to bed now?"

"Sure, son." He didn't look away.

"It's time for me to leave anyway." She twisted her wrist out of Gavin's grasp and stood, quickly gathering her bag and purse.

"Stick around, we need to talk." He pointed to the couch in a no-nonsense manner.

"Look, it's been a long day, I'm really tired. You must be, too." She raised her hands. "I'd like some time to clear my head before we talk more. OK?"

A silent, simmering shift just below the surface of his expression made her tense up. "You've had a lot more time to think about this than I have."

"I only found out on Wednesday."

"What'd you find out, Beth?" Patrick asked.

With the gravity of their situation, she'd forgotten Patrick was still in the room. What in the world should she tell him? "I just found out that your father is allergic to…ah…" Think of something. *Anything.* "Cats. Just like you. Only worse."

"Cats?" Patrick asked.

"Yeah. Highly allergic."

The boy's eyes grew huge and filled with tears. "I'm sorry, Dad. I didn't mean to…"

"What are you talking about Patrick?" Gavin asked.

The tears brimmed and spilled down Patrick's cheeks. "Mom got me a cat, and you got mad, and then you got divorced. I didn't know you were allergic."

Gavin darted to his side. "Son, you weren't the reason for our divorce. That was between Mommy and me." Patrick curled into his father's arms and Gavin gave Beth a pleading glance.

Great. She'd tried to put the kid off track and had only managed to upset him more. How was she to know they'd had an issue with a cat? Of all the luck.

"I'll leave you two alone," she said, taking her cue. "It sounds like you and I aren't the only ones with something to talk out."

"I have rounds in the morning." Gavin stood, holding Patrick close to his side and giving Beth a serious stare. "After that I'm taking Patrick to his soccer practice. And after that, you and I will talk."

CHAPTER FIVE

"PATRICK, what made you think Mommy and I got divorced because of you?" Gavin wrapped his arms around his son, who felt tiny and vulnerable, and squeezed him.

"You didn't come home sometimes, and Mommy got mad at me a lot."

"We were angry at each other, not at you, son." He kissed the top of Patrick's head, wishing things had been different.

Patrick looked up at him. "I heard her tell you on the phone she wanted to keep our cat not you. Then we moved away."

A strange stinging started behind Gavin's eyes. Patrick's precious face, along with its pained expression, blurred. His son had only been six when they'd gotten divorced, yet Patrick still re-membered a phone call and angry words, and above all he continued to feel sad about the breakup three years later. If he could only turn back the hands of time and fix things.

Gavin couldn't recall the last time he'd gotten all choked up. Had it been the day his son had been born? He may not have been around as much as he would have liked in Patrick's toddler years, but he still vividly remembered the wonder of seeing his son for the first time on the ultrasound and first touching him the day he'd been born. It had been the happiest day of his life. Right now he just wanted to hold Patrick and make all his sorrow go away. "No, son. You weren't to blame. Mommy and I sort of quit loving each other."

"Will you ever quit loving me?"

"No." Gavin gathered Patrick closer and the boy snuggled against his chest. "I'll always love you."

"No matter what?"

"No matter what."

"Good."

They stayed like that for several seconds, holding each other and breathing in sync, and Gavin tried to concentrate on his son and not the bombshell Beth had just dropped on him. Pregnant? Another child? Hell, he'd botched up enough with Patrick. How in the world would he handle another kid? "Anything else you want to talk about?"

"I miss my old friends. 'Specially Bobby. The kids here don't like me much."

"I know this is hard, Patrick, but I'll always be here for you. Why don't the kids like you?"

For the first time, Patrick smiled. "I can run faster and make more baskets."

Gavin grinned back. "Well, then, I'd say they're jealous and that's their problem, wouldn't you?"

"I guess."

"Isn't there anything you can all talk about?"

"Well, we all like the Lakers. They think my Kobe jersey is cool."

"There you go. You can talk about sports."

"I guess."

"And maybe we can invite Bobby to spend the weekend here some time."

"Cool!"

"Just promise me if you ever have anything on your mind, you'll come and talk to me about it."

Patrick's eyes drifted downward. "OK."

"Do you see a fracture?" The next morning, Gavin clipped an X-ray onto the glaring fluorescent view box for the other doctor to examine.

Julius White stopped studying his own films to help. He squinted and moved his face closer to the picture of the child's radius and ulna.

"Looks like a possible greenstick fracture right there." He pointed with a large finger to the spot.

Gavin grunted in agreement. "Hey, I didn't get a chance to tell you what a great job you did on that dog bite last week."

"Andrew. Yeah, that was interesting." Julius smiled at Gavin in the pitch-black radiology room. "Thanks, but it's what I get paid for." He continued to review his own series of X-rays beside Gavin. "So how'd the head of ER wind up with Sunday call?"

Gavin crossed his arms and stared at the films on the box. "Actually, it's only a half-day and I volunteered. I've got to give my residents some time off, you know."

"I hear you." Julius towered over Gavin's six-foot-one frame. He looked benignly downward at him and continued. "Andrew's father gave me some tickets for the Lakers game tonight. Since you were the admitting doctor, you want to go?"

Gavin gathered his X-rays up and began stuffing them back inside the file jacket. "Man, you know I'd love to, but I've got my son living with me now."

"Are you kidding me? It's the *Lakers*," Julius said in an incredulous tone. "And I've got sweet seats." His face seemed to question Gavin's sanity.

Gavin scratched his jaw. "It's awfully tempting but I'm going to be around for Patrick this time. He's at the age where he needs me more. I don't want to let him down again."

"I hear you. You're doing the right thing, man.

Listen, why don't you bring him along? I've got four seats, and McGuire can't go."

"Yeah, his wife had a baby on Friday night," Gavin said.

He'd made real progress with Patrick last night. When he looked into Patrick's eyes, he knew he was loved. There was no feeling like it. How could he refuse the Lakers, knowing how happy it would make Patrick?

Was he actually going to skip out on meeting Beth for a basketball game? Still flabbergasted over Bethany's news, he shook his head. What in the world would they do about it? She'd said she wanted to keep the baby, and didn't seem like the type to go after a guy for money, but he hardly knew her and didn't really have a clue what she might do. He needed to think things through and lay down some ground rules. He already had a kid. Was he ready for another?

Beth loomed over his conscience. He needed to face their situation head on.

"Listen, Julius, do you have anyone in mind for that fourth ticket?"

"I can think of ten people."

"The nurse I have in mind spent a lot of time with Andrew's sister that night."

Julius stopped staring at the X-rays and studied Gavin, as if remembering how guilty the teenage sister of his dog-bite patient felt. "If you want it, it's yours."

"Thanks, man. I owe you for that."

Gavin forced a smile and left Julius in the darkened radiology room. He headed back toward Emergency to question a father about how a two-year-old, for the second time in two months, had gotten another fracture that generally required twisting the arm. He suspected abuse and intended to inform the authorities.

Patrick ran up to his side, already dressed for soccer practice. "Are you almost done, Dad?" Once again he'd been left to hang out in the resident lounge with his book and a small hand-held electronic game.

"Half an hour." He dug into his pocket for some change. "Guess what?"

"What?"

"We're going to a basketball game tonight. The Lakers."

"The Lakers? Wow! Wait until the guys on the team hear this!"

"Here." He handed him some change. "Go get yourself a snack. No candy!" he called as he walked toward the patient room.

The boy nodded and ran off. Gavin felt as though he'd finally knocked down some of the walls between them. Far from being the trigger for the divorce, for the last year of their marriage Patrick had been the only reason they'd stayed together. Well, tonight they'd be the perfect father-son team and cheer their favorite LA team. And that would mark the beginning of their newer and better relationship.

And speaking of newer and better relationships, Gavin needed to make a call to ask Beth to the game. If Patrick was going to have a little sister or brother down the line, he may as well get used to being around Bethany now.

"I hear you did a great job at the homeless dinner on Saturday night," Ruth Caldwell said, looking pleased, from across the table in the Mexican restaurant.

"Yeah, I'm thinking I should get back to volunteering there more often."

"Great. As soon as my arthritis flare-up settles down, I'll be back. It lifts my spirits to help others."

Beth knew how much it meant to her mother to help those in need. After her father had died, Ruth had had to spend all her meager savings on the proper burial she'd insisted he have, and depended on the kindness of others to get by for everything else. The soup kitchen was her way of giving back.

"Have you heard from Neal lately, Beth, dear?" Ruth asked in a timid voice, forcing Beth out of her thoughts with the abrupt change in topic.

"Why would I hear from Neal, Mom?" Beth felt raw emotions threaten to get the best of her, but she fought them off. Or perhaps it was the pregnancy hormones. "We're divorced."

"Oh, you know me and my menopausal brain. I thought you two were still speaking to each other once in a while."

Beth tore at a corn tortilla and scooped up

some refried beans from her plate. Their marriage had ended on a sour note. She took a sip of iced tea and thought how much better off she was without her ex. "He's probably playing piano bar in a motel somewhere in Topeka with his new bimbo." She stuffed the food into her mouth. "Rest assured, we're never getting back together."

Her mother had obviously forgotten how devastated Beth had been when Neal had left for a gig one night and had never come home. Beth willed herself to humor her mother's amnesia over the lounge lizard that had once been her husband.

"I hear that handsome young doctor of yours caused quite a stir the other night."

Ah, so Mom was being coy about making sure Neal was definitely out of the picture before getting hopeful about a new man. Couldn't she just be direct and ask who the hunk was?

"Dr Riordan?" Two could play the coy game. "I helped him out with his son's allergies." She purposely left out the part about causing Gavin to have a systemic reaction. "I think he was just returning a favor."

"Sounds like he'll be helping out on a regular basis."

"Yes. He promised to provide fruit and vegetables every week and an occasional blood-pressure clinic. I hope you take advantage of it when he does."

"Nothing wrong with my blood pressure. Could you pass the salsa, please?"

Beth chomped down on a tortilla chip and waited for the right moment to approach a sensitive topic.

"Have you thought any more about moving into the senior housing unit?"

Ruth stopped the fork halfway to her mouth. "I'm only sixty-two. I'm not ready to give up my independence."

"You don't have to give up your independence to live there, Ma." Beth clasped her hair behind both ears and leaned forward, hoping her earnestness would come through. "You just won't have the burden of keeping up a yard, and house taxes, and all the other expenses of that old, drafty house of yours now that Dad's gone." She resorted to making the cajoling face she'd learned as a child. "And you wouldn't have to work any more, which means you could volunteer even more time." Beth scratched her nose. "Ma, you should at least go and look at one. You might be surprised." Her father had died suddenly four years before, leaving only a small insurance policy and an unpaid mortgage.

Ruth nibbled on a bit of rice. "I'll think about it."

They finished their lunch in silence. When the check came, Beth threw some money down and broached an even touchier subject. "Ma, do you need some cash? Are you OK until the first of the month?" She held three twenty-dollar bills in her hand in readiness.

Ruth eyed the cash with a look of shame. They both knew her job at the local department store chain didn't come close to covering her expenses. And the monthly social security check hardly made up for the rest. "It seems I am a little short again this month."

Beth passed the bills to her mom, who took them and patted her daughter's hand lovingly. "Thank you, Bethany, dear. What would I do without you?"

Beth took a deep breath and pushed down the heaviness that always seemed to sit on her chest when she dealt with her mother's stubbornness. Giving Ruth money always made her own funds dangerously low by month's end, but she never thought twice about helping out. It was a good thing she worked the two extra part-time jobs.

Now, however, with her pregnancy, she'd need to save all the extra money she could. Maybe she should look for a third job. Neal had bought himself and his girlfriend a whole new wardrobe using her charge cards, and had ruined her credit record. It was all Beth could do to pay off the interest on the card each month. The balance never seemed to change. But hiring a lawyer and pursuing the issue through the small claims court would only put her deeper in debt.

She'd learned her lesson, and she would never depend on a man again. Would Gavin offer to help out with the baby, or would she have to demand it? She'd find out more about where he stood on the issue when she saw him later today.

No one had been more surprised than Beth when Gavin told her he was taking her and Patrick to the Lakers Game that evening. More than pleased, she even wore purple in honor of the Los Angeles basketball team.

They entered the cavernous Staples Center to a whirr of noise, bright light and music so loud she couldn't hear herself think, let alone discuss anything personal with Gavin.

Patrick was so excited he could hardly contain himself. Gavin maintained a firm grasp on his shoulder to keep him from bouncing off the walls. And when Julius led them down, down and down almost to the main floor to where their seats were, she joined the excitement and had to pinch herself to make sure she hadn't gone to heaven.

What was Gavin's angle? Why invite her somewhere where it would be impossible to discuss their situation? Maybe it was more about being a gentleman. The tickets had fallen in his lap, and he hadn't wanted to stand her up. Could he be that considerate?

She glanced at him while he helped Patrick take off his jacket so his bright purple and gold jersey could be seen. Something about the tender gesture touched her heart. Gavin was a good man and father. Her pregnancy had been a surprise, but maybe she'd lucked out on Gavin being the father.

Looking at Patrick's bright eyes, and sensing her own enthusiasm about seeing her first live Lakers game, she let the pregnancy topic drop from her mind. She and Patrick high-fived and stomped their feet when the sports announcer welcomed the crowd to the game. Glancing around the arena, she realized she was surrounded by TV, movie, and pop stars, and worked hard not to stare. Patrick poked her in the ribs every time their team made a basket so she'd remember to jump up and cheer with him. She didn't have the heart to tell him she would have done it without his prodding.

Gavin grinned at her a lot, and she beamed back, thoroughly enjoying the game and the company.

During half-time, Julius offered to take Patrick to the concession stand for snacks. So far the evening had been going well. After they'd left, she gazed at Gavin, who had a hesitant look on his face, and she was reminded that theirs wasn't a normal date. They had a pressing topic to hash out. She tried not to let it ruin her fun night. As if reading her mind, he didn't broach the subject of her pregnancy. Instead of watching the cheerleading routine, they observed the crowd and talked about superficial things—anything to avoid the new and surprising bond between them.

After the game, Julius dropped everyone off at Gavin's house, where Beth had parked. Patrick had fallen asleep, and Gavin stood holding him in his arms in his driveway. She thanked both of the men profusely and attempted to make a quick getaway.

"Beth," Gavin called out in a strained whisper before she could take a step. "Why don't you come upstairs for a while?"

Julius gave a quick knowing glance at Beth, but

covered it well before he drove off. "I'll see you, man."

"Hey, thanks again, Jules."

Beth made a faux smile and swallowed back a sudden knot of nerves, then followed Gavin up the walkway.

Once he'd put Patrick to bed, he joined her in the huge Spanish-style living room. He got as far as the archway, snapped his fingers and trotted off to the kitchen. She heard water run and assumed he was filling the kettle. Her nerves jangled more. Rather than sit there and feel edgy, she followed him into the kitchen.

He'd taken two mugs from the cupboard, and turned and leaned his narrow hips against the counter. With folded arms and a decisive glance, he went straight to the point. "You laid some astounding news on me last night. I still don't know what to say."

"I'm still in shock, too." Her heart sped up, and she found it hard to meet his gaze.

"Have you changed your mind about keeping the baby?"

"No." Why would he ask that? Did he want her to end the pregnancy? Well, she wouldn't, not for him or anyone else.

After seeing her reaction, he scraped his jaw as if trying to think of a good way to say whatever else was on his mind. "Now, don't get upset, but I feel like I need to ask."

She straightened, cocked her head and trained a curious look his way, feeling the need to prepare for an insult.

He lifted his brows, and on an inhalation said, "Are you sure I'm the father?"

Anger flashed in her chest, accompanied by a rush of heat flaming up her neck and onto her cheeks. The kettle boiled and whistled. Ire sparked from her stare, which she flicked away from him while he poured steaming water over the teabags with a steady hand.

His accusation stung to her core. She counted to ten and tried to keep her voice down. "You're the only man I've been with since my divorce last year."

He stopped pouring and glanced at her.

"If you want to do a DNA test when the baby's born, it's fine with me." She brushed him off with a wave of the hand.

He dipped a teabag and handed her the mug. "Look, I didn't mean to insult you."

She took it, biting her lip. Strained silence ensued while they both pretended to be unnaturally interested in their tea.

OK, she'd give him the benefit of the doubt. He wasn't running away from the situation, he was just asking the questions foremost on his mind. Gavin needed to wrap his brain around the situation just as much as she did. She blew over her mug and took a tentative sip. After composing herself, she searched for an excuse to leave.

He looked uncomfortable, as if he'd give anything to take back what he'd insinuated, but she wasn't ready to let him off the hook.

"If you don't mind," she said, "I'm really tired and should be going now."

He stared at her in deep thought, his lips drawn into a straight line. "Then we'll talk more about this soon."

Dreading another awkward conversation with Gavin, she took one more sip of tea and handed him the mug. "I guess it's something we can't avoid. But, listen, thanks for asking me to the game tonight. Despite the last fifteen minutes, I've had a good time."

Tension broke from his face. "I'm glad I did something right." He smiled. "You're welcome."

She nodded, softening the slightest bit. "Patrick's a great kid."

"Agreed."

When they reached the front door, Beth turned quickly and said goodnight.

Gavin nodded and reiterated, "We'll talk more soon."

As she walked to her car, she went over his words. He'd said he hadn't meant to insult her, but he sure as hell had.

On Monday morning, Beth dove right into work and tried to keep Gavin out of her mind. Would he ever think of their baby in the same way he thought about his son?

Doubt ushered in a wave of anxiety. First she had to make it through the first trimester. So far, so good. Other than being tired and having mild morning sickness, she hadn't had anything to worry about. No spotting. No cramping. Nothing unusual.

Beth finished the last intradermal injection of venom into the soft skin of the inside of her patient's forearm. Her forty-year-old male patient had been stung by something three weeks ago. The reaction had been fierce. His face and neck had swollen up and he'd become dizzy, according to the history on his chart.

Now it was Beth's job to discover which stinging insect it might have been by giving him incremental injections of diluted venom from the honeybee, yellow jacket, wasp, white-faced hornet and yellow hornet. So far he hadn't reacted to the lower dilutions. The trick was to catch any response before it had a chance to spread to full-blown anaphylaxis. She eyed the quick-acting antihistamine and vial of epinephrine in readiness nearby.

Dr Mehta tapped Beth on the shoulder.

"Yes?" She turned her head toward her boss.

"They want you in the emergency room. A teenager needs asthma training."

"Why didn't they ask the nurse educator?"

"Dr Riordan specifically asked for you," Dr Mehta said. "Go ahead. I'll have one of the other nurses finish up here."

What was Gavin up to now?

She went to the cupboard for the training tray filled with demonstration inhalers and grabbed some literature and a video aimed at teenagers with asthma.

A few minutes later she knocked on the door to the emergency room and peered through the thick plate-glass window. Without the code, she couldn't let herself in. Carmen pushed something under the counter, the door buzzed and opened, and she waved her in. Beth approached the tall nurse feeling a bit unsure. Did Carmen know she was pregnant? And if she did know, would she put two and two together and deduce that Gavin was the father?

"The kid is in room five." Carmen's shrill

voice cut through the noise. She motioned for Beth to come closer. "He's been in here four or five times in the last two months. Totally non-compliant." She squinted and spoke intently. "Gavin's afraid he'll just ignore us if we send him to another department for retraining." Carmen forced an unnatural smile. "He decided to bring the mountain to Mohammed," she said, giving Beth the once-over and chuckling at an apparent private joke. "Or, in your case, it's more like a hill than a mountain."

Beth took the chart from Carmen's hand and read: "Mohammed Jackson, 18 y/o African-American male. Admitting diagnosis: uncontrolled asthma."

She strode across the ER to the room while preparing what she intended to say to the patient. At that exact moment, as if by radar, Gavin backed out of the adjacent room in mid-sentence about the need for a spinal tap.

"Excuse me just a second," he said to the family in the room. "Why don't you talk it over, and I'll be right back?" He snagged Beth's hand

and led her back to the nurses' station. "Let me fill you in on Mohammed." He nodded toward room five where the patient waited, and stared into her eyes as though nothing bad had happened last night. "He's laid down so much scar tissue from not treating his asthma that his lung capacity is probably three-quarters of what it should be for a guy his age. I wanted to admit him to the hospital, but he refuses." He gave Beth a tense smile. "You're my last hope. You did great with Patrick the other night, and you know how to work with teenagers, and I figure Mohammed may listen to a pretty woman more than a hairy guy like me."

"Why didn't you call the respiratory therapy educator?"

"Because I wanted you." He stared deeper into her eyes for a few intense seconds, sending a blood rush from her head to her toes. He wanted her. "To explain things to him. And when you're done, I need to talk to you again."

He didn't give her a chance to respond before he walked away.

"Well, speaking of non-compliant, have you gotten your EpiPen yet?" she called after him. He ignored her. It figured.

Beth had to gather her thoughts after Gavin had blown her off course. She wanted to hold onto her anger, but being around him made it almost impossible. He was simply looking out for one of his patients. She stood outside the patient room and read the chart.

"Gavin?" Carmen called out.

"Yo."

"The possible appendicitis is next."

He took the chart she handed to him and asked, "Is it my imagination, or is it extra busy for a Monday morning?"

"It's always busy in the ER," Carmen sang. "You know the motto—treat and street. Now, hop to it!"

"Yes, ma'am." Off he went.

Beth entered the room, introduced herself, and did a quick patient assessment. She extended her hand to shake his. A lanky arm connected to an IV cautiously took it.

Beanpole thin in the hospital gown, Mohammed

looked younger than his age. An IV piggyback of cortisol was connected to the main IV to help decrease the inflammation in his lungs. A small machine delivered medication to open his airway through a long thick tube and mouthpiece. So Respiratory Therapy had already been here. Gavin really hadn't needed to send for her.

The patient "sipped" every few seconds on the nebulized medicine coming from the contraption as if smoking a peace pipe then held his breath and coughed, repeating the process over and over. He knew the routine.

"I gather you've been having some trouble with your asthma," she said. "Thought I might find out how we can help you today."

Gavin tried to conceal his interest in room five after he'd examined his latest patient and ordered a batch of lab tests. He'd hurt Beth's feelings and it ate at him. He needed to set things straight. He pretended to be involved in reading the chart in his hand while thinking things through.

Carmen took it from him, turned it right side

up and gave it back. "You might be able to read it better this way."

What could he do but grin?

He handed Carmen some doctor's orders and walked to the other side of the counter where he shuffled through more papers before sneaking a peek at room five, again.

Shortly, Beth emerged from the patient's room looking victorious, and Gavin was the lucky recipient of her gorgeously broad smile. Maybe things were looking up.

"How did it go?" he asked.

"Really well." Pride beamed in her eyes.

Gavin liked that look. He liked it so much he had to shove his hands in his white coat pockets to prevent himself grabbing and planting a deep kiss on her, before asking for her forgiveness. Instead, he smiled sedately.

They stood by the nurses' station, grinning awkwardly at each other for a few seconds, until Carmen interrupted.

"Oh, for crying out loud, people. This is a hospital, not reality TV."

With a bright blush on her cheeks, Bethany said, "Mohammed said he'd give the new medical regimen a try."

"How'd you do that?"

"I told him you would foot the bill for all the meds." She winked at Gavin, gathered her tray and tried to leave the ER.

He snagged her arm, led her into his office and closed the door. Once inside, he motioned for her to sit. He sat on the edge of his desk to be close to her.

"I need to apologize for what I said last night. It didn't come out right."

She still looked ticked off, with the foot of her crossed leg pumping up and down. "If it's money you're worried about, don't. I won't bleed you dry. But with diapers, formula, clothes…" She sighed. "I would appreciate help with half of the expenses."

"Of course I won't let you bear the brunt of what we did together." He reached out and touched her shoulder. "The thing is, I hardly know you—not that I don't like what I do know about you, but it's a totally new situation and it all seems so unreal." Was he over-explaining?

She softened the slightest bit, but wouldn't look into his eyes. "I know."

"We did use contraception."

She slumped in her chair the tiniest bit. "You and I both know condoms are the best option for STD protection, but the statistics are not so great for birth control."

He nodded. She definitely had a point. Again, poor judgement. "For what it's worth, I wouldn't change what happened that night. I'd rather you hadn't gotten pregnant, but I'm not going to let you go through this alone. I want you to see Karen Scott, the best OB doctor at Mercy. Her panel is completely full, but she'll see you if I ask."

Finally, she glanced cautiously at him. Their eyes locked. "Thank you for that. But I should tell you that I've gotten this far along in a pregnancy before when I was married, and I wound up miscarrying."

"Oh, Beth, I'm so sorry." Gavin wanted to

reach out to her, to touch her hand or shoulder, to find some way of consoling her, but held back. He couldn't imagine losing a baby, or the devastation it would cause. With an intense desire to alleviate her pain, he only managed to come up with something superficial and lame. "That was probably a fluke. You know, nature taking care of itself."

"Twice?"

They stared at each other. She dared him to come up with another pat answer with eyes so tinged with pain he felt his heart squeeze.

"In a few weeks all of our worrying may be for nothing," she said, resignation coloring her tone.

Wanting to shout, *No! We'll make this pregnancy work, no matter what,* he kept his mouth firmly shut. She'd lost not one but two babies and, as little as he knew about her, he could tell it had left a deep scar. How could it not? He wanted to take her in his arms and comfort her, stroke her hair and assure her that all would be well this time around. How irrational was that with a woman he hardly knew? So he'd help the best way he could. "That's all the more reason to get in to see Karen as soon as possible. I'll call her today."

Her normally bright hazel eyes remained clouded and sad. And he hadn't helped her current problem a bit by asking her to verify last night that he was the father. A strange dull ache made him scratch his chest. "Regardless of what happens, I'd like to get to know you better. Would that be OK with you?"

She looked taken aback, her eyes widened and her cheeks tinted a pleasant shade of pink. "I suppose so."

"Patrick has karate tomorrow afternoon and, after that, music lessons, which gives me a few free hours. Can you spare some time for me then?"

If the look on her face was any indication, he was about to hear another inventive excuse for getting out of spending time alone with him. "If you want to tag along with me while I make some deliveries."

"Deliveries? Like pizza?"

"Not even funny, Riordan. It's another part-time job. Why don't you come along and find out? We can talk while I drive."

Gavin watched a twenty-year-old, nondescript four-door sedan drive to his curb. It looked clean and functional, sort of like its owner, only if you added the terms sleek and alluring. He smiled and felt a buzz of excitement as she neared the driveway. It seemed curiously sexy, knowing Beth carried his child. Nah, he was *not* turned on about that.

She smiled and waved him in. He opened the door to myriad aromas. The back of the car was filled with a large hot box.

"You do deliver pizza." Gavin glanced toward the backseat, wondering where her hat was.

"Nope. Senior nutrition service. For those who hate to cook, we deliver." Beth sparkled a smile his way.

"Another volunteer job?" He raised a brow. "You'll never get rich like that."

"Actually, it's a part-time job, every other Tuesday afternoon, and I get paid." She looked him directly in the eye then quickly back to the road. "Though not much."

He shook his head. "You could make a hell of a lot more money working one extra shift a week in the ER instead of all of these weird little jobs."

"I don't do ER. When my stress level rises, my IQ drops. And I can't take blood and guts. Besides, I like my 'weird little jobs'. It's my way of giving back to the community."

How was it he'd never met a woman like her before? He glanced across the car and saw a fresh-scrubbed complexion and hair silken and shiny. She was wearing it down and he had an urge to run his fingers through it.

"So where's your delivery hat?"

She rolled her eyes and ignored him. He finally fastened his seat belt and placed his arm along the bench seat. He left it dangerously close to her tempting hair. He itched to tickle and play with the honey-colored ends.

He propped his ankle on the adjacent knee. "What's for dinner?"

"For us or them?" Bethany concentrated on the road ahead.

An impulse had him snag a lock of hair and twist it around his finger. "Why don't you tell me both and I'll decide if I want to eat with you or the seniors." He tugged affectionately. She pulled away the slightest bit, so he let go.

"Well," she said. "Inside the delivery box you'll find some kosher meals and a few chicken Parmesan, boiled potatoes and mixed vegetable meals. Since I owe you dinner, I'm giving you the choice between the Weiner Haven or Ted's Charbroiled Burgers." She tossed him an apologetic look. "It's all I can afford until Friday."

Payday. He thought of a cozy Italian place where they could sit knee to knee and gaze into each other's eyes while sharing a plate of spaghetti, but Beth wanted to repay him the dinner she owed him and had made it clear she was short on cash. "I've been craving a double cheese burger for days," he said. "Definitely Ted's."

She grinned and switched on the radio to country music. It figured that songs about love, family, and life's simple pleasures would appeal to her. Slowly, the puzzle that was Beth began to materialize and he enjoyed connecting the pieces.

Gavin insisted on being useful and accompanied Beth to the door with the first of several deliveries. He acted the part of waiter and placed each covered dish before the older couples as they smiled and looked on.

By the last house, Gavin was thoroughly into his delivery-boy persona. He hopped out of the car and carried the warm platter on the tips of all five fingers, above his head. If he'd had a large cloth napkin, it would have been slung over his arm.

He insisted on knocking. The door rattled. Bethany stood at his side and grinned at him. He winked at her and looked forward to stealing a kiss later. No one answered. He knocked harder and Bethany called out the lady's name. Still no answer.

"That's odd." She walked to a front window, cupped her hands and looked inside. "Mrs Harrington uses a walker—maybe she's just taking longer than usual?"

Gavin opened the screen and tried the handle

on the door. It was locked. He led Beth around the side of the house to the back. He tapped on the door and called out her name. The door wasn't locked.

"Mrs Harrington?" He opened it wider.

They ventured inside and walked toward the kitchen. He put the meal on the table and explored deeper inside the house. "Mrs Harrington? It's the dinner service."

They heard a weak cat-like mew and rushed toward a closed door off the dining room. A bathroom. Bethany edged the door open and found the walker on its side just out of Mrs Harrington's reach. Now doubled over on the toilet, whimpering, the elderly woman had managed to hit her head at some point. Dried blood caked on the floor.

"Can you help me?" a shaky, frail voice pleaded.

Bethany rushed to her side and checked her pulse. "How long have you been here?" She checked her over from head to toe.

"I can't remember."

"Did you lose consciousness?"

"I don't think so." She reached with trembling arms for Beth's hands.

"Squeeze," she said, testing for signs of a stroke.

Gavin had been waiting at the door to give the woman privacy, but quickly strode inside to lift her from the toilet. She wore pajamas and had probably been stuck there since the night before. Paper-thin skin showed a freeway of red capillaries and blue vessels. It wouldn't take much to tear her skin and make her bleed. They needed to be extra careful. Her feet were blue from poor circulation and blood pooling with gravity. Even though a deadweight, she was light when he lifted and carried her into the bedroom after Bethany had pulled her pajama bottoms up.

"I'm a doctor. Can you feel anything in your legs?" he asked when she felt like ice.

Beth rushed into the bedroom with a damp washcloth and dabbed at the cut outlined with dried blood on the woman's forehead.

"I feel pins and needles."

"Move your toes for me," he said. "Good." He watched Beth tend to the woman, gently pinching the flesh on her arm, which stayed peaked. "Poor skin turgor. She's badly dehydrated. I'll call for an ambulance. She needs IV fluids." She picked up the phone at the bedside.

"You'll be fine." Gavin made a point of reassuring the woman. "We're going to get some medical attention for you, OK?"

She nodded approval as if she were a limp, antique rag doll.

Later, with their plans thrown off course by the paramedics' visit, Gavin suggested they get the burgers from Ted's as take-out. "I know a spot with a great view, Beth. And it's near Patrick's karate studio. Let's eat there."

"Fine with me, as long as it's not too far. I'm starving."

She looked so cute in faded jeans and a blue shirt that if his hands hadn't been full of hamburgers and drinks, he would have scooped her into his arms and squeezed her. She had a sweet way of lifting herself up onto her toes when she walked, a jaunty step that made it extra fun to follow behind.

Back in the car, he directed her up several long, winding roads to the lookout point he had in mind. "You say you don't like working in the ER, but back at Mrs Harrington's you showed all the signs of a great triage nurse."

"Not really. What I did was just common sense."

"That's exactly what a good triage nurse needs. And don't underestimate yourself. You're a good nurse."

Once they'd arrived at the lookout point, they parked and sat on the hood of her car. He used the windshield as a backrest, and tore open his bag. "I did good, right?"

"Oh, Gavin, the view is wonderful. I never knew this place existed." She sat straight, her back slightly arched with her hands on her knees, feet on the bumper, scanning the panoramic vista of twilight with glittering dots and long flowing streams of car lights below. The early moon hung just above her head in a perfect half-circle. A breeze gently lifted her hair.

The view was spectacular, and seemed close enough to touch. He hated to tear his gaze away from Beth to look at the city. After they ate, he checked his watch. In twenty minutes he'd have to leave to pick up Patrick. He clasped his hands behind his head and tried to remember when he had last felt this relaxed. Beth leaned back on one arm and twisted to look at him.

"Come here," he said.

She crawled up the hood and sat beside him. Spending the last few hours with her, coupled with their medical adventure, had him feeling like they were old friends. He put his arm around her and pulled her near. She didn't resist.

"We make a great team, eh?"

She nodded. "Poor Mrs Harrington. What would have happened if we hadn't come along?"

"Good question. I guess we were meant to be there." He played with her hair. "Hey, I made an appointment with Dr Scott for you this Thursday."

"Great. Thanks."

Things got quiet as they pondered the meaning of her first obstetrics appointment. They'd made a baby together, a beautiful thing. He glanced at her and felt a surge of affection. Even though unexpected, making a baby with Bethany *was* a beautiful thing.

"Tell me about your marriage," he said, curious to know how she'd been hurt. It had to be the key to why she was so cautious with him.

As if checking his sincerity, she gazed into his eyes, hers more green today than hazel. "I swear to you, this isn't a pattern, but we had to get married. I thought I loved him, but everything went wrong from the start. After my second miscarriage, I lost all hope. Then he left me for someone else."

"What a bastard."

"You've got that right."

"How did he feel about losing the babies?"

Her shoulders slumped. "I honestly don't think he cared."

How could she trust another man after that? God, he wanted to hold her. To offer the kind of comfort she deserved. No wonder she expected him to be a heel, too. And to think he'd practically accused her of having several affairs by asking if he was the only possible father. "Oh, honey." He pulled her closer. "That stinks."

He felt her tense up, as though she didn't want to talk about her failed marriage another second. Maybe by sharing his own divorce story, he could keep their new-found lines of communication open, and he could get her to trust him. "I don't know about you, but I felt damn bitter after my divorce."

"Bitter doesn't come close to how I felt."

"I found it hard to pick up and carry on," he said.

"I wanted to sleep twenty-four hours a day, but I had a job to do and obligations to my patients."

"Sometimes that's a good thing," he said. "You know, life must go on and all that."

She clicked her tongue. "And look where we've wound up."

He gave a wry laugh. She had a point.

"What went wrong with your marriage?" she asked.

"A better question would be what *didn't* go wrong."

This time she laughed, and it made him feel good to lighten her mood, even at his own expense.

"Well, Patrick certainly was a gift," she said.

"Yes. Definitely. It tore me up to lose him. I hated it. I was doing the best I knew how, and Maureen was pushing all of my buttons. And she dangled Patrick like a carrot so I'd ante up. How could she treat our son like that? And then, three years after the divorce, just when we were all getting used to how things were going, she took off for England and pulled the poor kid out of his school to live with me."

Bethany's hand warmed his. A look of complete understanding settled in her eyes. It gave him the courage to open up more.

"If it hadn't been for my med school debts, I would have fought harder for custody, but everyone sided with Maureen and said it was in Patrick's best interests to be with his mom." He shook his head. "Now that I have him back, even though it's only temporary, I don't ever want to be out of his life again." He stared deeply into her eyes. "What I'm trying to say is I'm not going to abandon the baby."

There it was again, that incredible smile that only she could make. It made him want to grab her. He knew he had to leave soon, but couldn't resist. He reached for her and gave her a different kind of kiss—more like long-term lovers sharing a moment of deep affection. She reached around his neck and held him firmly in place to deepen the kiss. He liked that. Hell, he liked her. He rubbed and massaged her back and arms—soft and warm. A wave of heat washed over him like a soothing blanket.

He brushed some of her hair away and studied her lovely, expressive eyes, her cheeks, and delicately shaped lips. Perhaps he stared too long.

Like a shy kid, she cuffed his shoulder. "Stop looking at me like that."

"How am I looking at you?"

"Like you think I'm freaky or strange or…"

"Or beautiful?"

She grew still. "Must be that glow of motherhood."

That forced his mind back to their situation. "Just to let you know. Every minute I spend with you, I like you more. I wish things were different, but I'm willing to explore the possibility of you and me."

She relaxed against him. "It's so strange, isn't it? I mean, how do you start to date a guy who is already the father of your child?"

He tilted his head back and gave a wry laugh. "I guess we'll have to figure it out as we go along." He checked his watch. "In the meantime, I've got to pick up Patrick."

They broke apart with regret and he hopped off the car and helped her down. "I was thinking about asking Carmen to babysit Patrick on Saturday night so I can take you to a special Italian place I know."

"Oh. Um. I'm sorry, but I can't." She wiped her hands on her jeans.

"Ah, come on, is it another part-time job?"

"No. I have a date."

CHAPTER SIX

GOOD old Larry from the lab. How long ago had they made their plans for the west coast version of that hit Broadway musical? Long before Beth had known Gavin even existed. If the tickets for the musical hadn't been so damn expensive, she'd consider calling it off. But she couldn't do that to Larry, they'd been friends too long.

Beth bashed the steering-wheel with the cuff of her hand as she drove away from Gavin's house.

She'd never forget the look on Gavin's face when she'd said no to his offer of dinner on Saturday night. If only she'd said no the night they'd met, they wouldn't be in this predicament. But then she would never have had the chance to get to know him, and so far she liked what she'd found out about him just fine.

She shook her head. To his credit, Gavin did seem to be trying to venture into a possible relationship with her. And what was it with him about getting her to consider working in the ER as a triage nurse? That was the last place she belonged. Especially as he worked there! Though he did have a point about her being able to earn a lot more money working the ER than at the teen clinic and delivering meals on wheels combined.

Where the baby was concerned, it was crunch time, and the need to stay on top of things would have to be taken into account in any decisions. And she had to admit she'd gotten a tiny rush of adrenaline and a sense of really being connected with her community when they'd rescued Mrs Harrington. But the lady had already quit bleeding! A little voice in the back of her head suggested that most of the people who came to the ER weren't actively bleeding either. OK, so maybe she'd think about it.

Beth smiled, and remembered their tender kiss on the hood of her car. How romantic was that?

She liked Gavin. She *really* liked him. Talk about chemistry. Yes, she was sounding dangerously similar to a teenager with a crush, with one exception—she happened to be carrying his baby. He'd given his word to help out with bringing a child into the world, had even arranged for a top-notch doctor to be her OB specialist, but what about personal commitment?

Gavin was obviously making up for lost time with his son, and the boy deserved nothing less, so how would she and a baby fit into the picture? And if they did get involved, would he lose interest in her and move on like her ex-husband had? Regardless, Beth would never admit it to him, could hardly admit it to herself, but she'd be counting the days until Saturday. Thank goodness he'd invited her to Patrick's soccer game on Saturday afternoon as a substitute for dinner.

Rubbing her stomach, feeling a glimmer of hope that things might work out for the best, she turned the corner and headed for home.

* * *

Some time around four o'clock on Thursday afternoon, Gavin appeared in the testing lab of the allergy department. Beth looked up and froze. She had been in the middle of three different skin tests, running between curtains and gurneys, checking skin reactions on patients' backs and setting clocks to time others. She looked at his serious expression and shrank back.

He stood there, his hands on his hips. "Do you have a minute?"

"It's a little hectic right now." Not that she didn't have an urge to drop everything for the man who, just by showing up, made her feel weak in the knees.

He approached, touched her elbow. "Thirty seconds," he said, and led her to the corner of the room.

Her heart thumped in her chest. She made one guess at why was he there.

"How did the appointment go with Karen?" he whispered.

Surprised, but pleased he'd remembered her first OB doctor's appointment, she answered,

"Really well. She said I was about six weeks along and could expect to deliver in December."

Dr Scott had assured Beth that at twenty-eight she was in great shape and she shouldn't worry about miscarrying. It was enough to keep Beth optimistic that she'd actually go through the whole pregnancy this time. Deep in her heart she didn't think she could survive losing another baby.

"December. Huh. That's great," he said, seeming to relax a bit and almost smiling. "A Christmas baby…just like me."

"Really?" Why did that bit of information, something as simple as a father and child sharing the same birth month, kindle a secret ember of hope? Her hormones must be running amok with her emotions.

He nodded, and dug into his white coat pocket. "Here." He thrust a bag at her. When she looked inside she saw three bottles of prenatal vitamins. "Be sure to take these every day. That should last you awhile."

How sweet of him. She didn't have the heart

to tell him she'd already filled a prescription from Dr Scott. Feeling a new and positive spin on their circumstances, she almost kissed his cheek, but remembered, just in time, where she was. He'd come all the way up from the ER to ask about her appointment and to give her vitamins. Downright charming. If that didn't prove he cared about the pregnancy, what did?

On a whim she asked, "Would you like to come to my next appointment? Dr Scott is going to do an ultrasound."

His expression shifted from surprise to contemplation to a smile. "You know, I think I would."

"Great. It's the Thursday after next at two."

"I'll put it on my calendar."

A timer went off, and a patient called out, "Nurse?"

"I'll be right there," she answered, and turned back to Gavin, whispering, "And I'll see you on Saturday around noon."

He smiled, put his hands in his pockets and brushed by on his way toward the exit. "See you then."

She inhaled and savored his woodsy after-shave. "Hey, Dr Riordan?" she called.

He stopped and turned.

"When are you planning to start your allergy shots?"

He shrugged. "Next week?"

"Sounds good." She heard another timer go off, then remembered one more thing. "Have you picked up your EpiPen yet?"

He'd already pushed through the clinic doors.

Beth arrived at Gavin's house as planned at noon on Saturday. He opened the door with a big smile, wearing a T-shirt and sports shorts showing off muscular legs lightly dusted with hair. She tried not to ogle him, and was glad to be wearing sunglasses, but he looked fantastic and the man deserved a little admiration.

"Hey," he said. "Come in while I get Patrick organized." He stepped back from the door to allow her to enter, and gave her a quick once-over. It was the first time he'd ever seen her in shorts, too.

The fact that her breasts had really blossomed with her pregnancy hadn't gone unnoticed. She felt suddenly shy and adjusted the brim on her ball cap and ran her hand over her ponytail.

Gavin, battling over staring too long, made a poor attempt to look into her eyes. He cleared his throat. "You look really hot today."

Warmth sprang to her cheeks. "Thanks." She was glad she'd chosen a buttercup yellow top and khaki shorts instead of the cropped pants she'd considered.

He cupped his hand to his mouth and called down the hall. "Patrick!" He glanced back at Beth. "That kid. I swear he stays holed up in his room every chance he gets. Patrick? He doesn't have a computer in there either. I won't let him."

Beth heard a door slam and clumpy footsteps trotting along the hardwood hallway floor.

Patrick soon appeared dressed for his soccer match mildly breathless with a bright smile on his face. "Hi, Beth."

"Hey."

"And where are your shinguards?" Gavin asked.

The boy looked surprised that he'd forgotten. He coughed.

"Go back and get your equipment. And hurry so we won't be late for warm-up."

"OK." He gave another dry cough, and ran off.

Gavin and Beth smiled at each other while they waited.

"So, you all ready for your big date tonight?" he teased.

She lifted her chin. "As a matter of fact, I'm looking forward to it."

"I bet you are."

A few seconds later Patrick was back with everything he needed. "I'm all set, Dad. Can we get pizza after the game?"

Beth heard a familiar sound as he spoke and went on alert. She'd heard the same wheezy tone in many a child with asthma when it first started to tighten the airway.

"We'll see," Gavin answered.

Patrick coughed again.

"Have you used your inhaler today?" she asked.

"This morning."

"What was your peak-flow reading?"

"Almost 300."

"Do you feel like you could blow that now?"

"Maybe. I dunno."

"You think you might need your rescue inhaler? I'm pretty sure that's wheezing I'm hearing."

"I'm OK."

"Listen to the lady. She can tell you're wheezing. Go and use your inhaler. Scoot. And bring it with you!" Gavin lifted his palms and gave Beth a baffled look. "He was fine all morning."

"Does he always keep his bedroom door closed? Have you been in there lately?"

"I go in there all the time but, to be honest, I think he's hiding something from me."

"Hmm."

Patrick appeared before they could finish the conversation. Beth watched him take a puff from his inhaler through a clear tubular aerochamber then they all walked to the car, loaded everything up, and a few minutes later he took the second puff. Within minutes Beth could hear a difference with his breathing. Patrick obviously felt it too, and talked non-stop all the way to the soccer field, not showing the slightest hint of being breathless.

An hour and a half later, Patrick's team screamed and yelled, jumping up and down with their victory. After non-stop running she'd expect them to show signs of fatigue, but the boys seemed more pumped up than they had been before the game had started.

"Check it out." Gavin grinned and pointed. "Patrick told me he wasn't making any new friends, but look at that." Patrick and a group of four boys had put their arms around each other and walked to the sideline as if they were long-lost buddies.

A few minutes later, when the cheers and screams had died down, he came running up to Gavin. "Can I get pizza with Chad and Matt? Their mom asked if I could go. Can I?"

"Sure. Let me talk to her."

While Gavin spoke to the boy's mother, Patrick fidgeted. "Did you see me score that goal?"

"I sure did. You were great." She glanced down

and saw unabashed pride on his face. It touched her heart. She ruffled his flyaway hair and he pretended to be annoyed but didn't move away. The child must really miss his mother. Bending down, she cupped his cheeks with her palms and kissed him smack in the middle of his forehead. He looked surprised, but didn't fight it.

"Are you going to be my dad's girlfriend?"

She sighed. "I'm not sure what I'm going to be, Patrick. But one thing is certain. I'd like to be your friend."

"OK."

"Any more wheezing?"

He stopped, put his grimy hand on his chest, and took a deep breath. "Nope. I'm good."

"That's great. Now, go and enjoy your pizza." He ran off, leaving a distinct sweaty boy scent. "And have a piece for me!"

Gavin willed himself to behave, and not bowl Bethany over with his strong desire for her. They'd sat thigh to thigh all afternoon and, frankly, it was very tough to act like a gentleman.

Still, he'd promised himself he'd behave. But somewhere between walking from his car to her doorstep, and definitely some time after she'd gotten out of her own car, he forgot every one of his resolutions. He'd followed her home. Maybe that hadn't been such a great idea.

He'd blame his heightened desire on her slim, though shapely legs and that jaunty walk of hers as she trotted up her front steps to open the door. Being around her felt as natural as breathing. He hadn't felt the need to entertain her. He'd felt perfectly at ease, except for when their thighs had touched when they'd sat on the bleachers. He'd been completely fine with mundane conversation. The fact was, he felt very comfortable with Beth.

When he caught up to her on the porch, he swept her through the door, kicked it shut, and ravished her with a deep kiss. He danced her backwards around the room, showering her with kisses, caresses and whispered words. She giggled and half-heartedly protested, but that only spurred him on.

He would have continued to nip and nibble her

ear and neck and jaw and lips had he not had the sudden need to…

He turned his head, covered his mouth—and sneezed. "Excuse me!" He sneezed again.

A pudgy gray tabby looked up drowsily from the couch to see where the noise was coming from.

"Are you OK?" Bethany asked.

"The cat." He pointed.

She rushed to the kitchen on the other side of an open bar and rummaged through a cupboard for a bottle, snatched up a tissue, returned and handed both to him.

"Thanks." He popped open the bottle and put a pill under his tongue.

"You really are allergic to cats?"

He shrugged. "I didn't know."

"You keep the bottle," she said.

Nodding, he made his best effort at a smile before blowing his nose.

"Would you like some lemonade?"

"Sure." He'd gladly suffer from an allergy to cats and agree to anything to stay in her company longer. He scanned the tiny living room, admiring her simplicity in decoration and the homey effect. "You've got a nice place here."

"It's a postage stamp compared to your house," she said from the kitchen. "But I think it's cozy."

He went to the door, leaned on the frame, and looked into what could only be described as a kitchenette. "It's very…quaint." How would she have room for a baby here?

"Precisely." Beth smiled while she poured their drinks.

Her cat paced back and forth by his leg, rubbing its side against his calf. He fought back another sneeze and dabbed at his watering eyes. "You know you need to be careful changing his litter-box while you're pregnant."

"I know, Doc. Toxoplasmosis. Don't worry, I wear a mask."

He distracted himself by once again checking out her great legs, really pleased she'd worn shorts that day. She handed him a glass with a hand-painted lemon on it and led him back to the other room.

"Are you going to be able to do this?" She gestured toward her cat.

"I'm tough."

They plopped down onto a couch and drank lemonade, making eye contact over the rims of their glasses. Bethany grinned and accidentally dribbled on her chin.

"Oh, gosh, excuse me." She used the back of her hand to wipe her jaw. "I'm such a slob."

"Hardly." Gavin put down his glass and moved closer, putting his arm around her. "I had a great time today. And I know Patrick liked having you there."

"I liked being there, too. Thanks for inviting me."

Spending the afternoon with Bethany at his son's soccer game had been fantastic. He wanted to keep seeing her, to get a sense of how things might play out. He also wanted to make love to her again. Soon. He rubbed her shoulder and drew her closer.

But, damn it all, he couldn't just have her over to spend the night, not with Patrick being so inquisitive. And it wouldn't be right to palm Patrick off on Carmen just so he could spend the night here. Being a single father made things so complicated.

They'd have to get creative and steal time to be together—that was, if Beth wanted to be with him as much as he wanted to be with her.

What if things didn't work out? Patrick really liked Beth and he would have to suffer through the breakup, too. With all the changes his son was dealing with, Gavin couldn't justify adding one more hitch. But the fact remained that he wanted to spend more time with Beth.

Then he remembered Beth had a date tonight anyway. Some lucky guy would get to spend the whole evening with her, and it bugged the hell out of him.

"What do I have to do to compete with this other guy?"

She gave a coy smile. "Nothing. He's just a friend." She took off her ball cap. "He was there for me after the breakup with my husband and all through the divorce." She played with her ponytail and stared at the coffee table. "Like I said, we're just friends."

Right. Like men knew how to be friends with women. "Trust me, whoever he is, he isn't thinking friendship when he's looking into your pretty eyes." He knew how guys thought. Friendship with a young attractive woman was impossible unless, of course… "Unless he's gay, he's waiting for the right time to make his move. I guarantee it."

She frowned her disbelief. He edged closer.

"Is he someone from the hospital I might know?"

"Maybe. He's the evening supervisor for the laboratory."

"Larry, the lab guy—Rossmore?"

"That would be him."

Tall. Skinny. Long hair that had never seen the inside of a salon.

Gavin took Beth by the shoulders and turned her toward him. "When Larry tries to kiss you tonight, and I know he will, I want you to remember this." He leaned in and planted a soft, loving kiss on her lips. She took a deep breath as he moved closer and kissed her fully. His tongue ventured across her lips, into her mouth. She tasted sweet and tart, like lemonade. He found her tongue and toyed with it. She joined in the dance.

Her arms tightened around his neck. Obviously, she liked what he was doing. He decided to check out her pregnancy-enhanced breasts. Nice. Perfect for his hand. A quick sweep of his thumb across her nipple proved she liked his touch. He tightened his hold and deepened the kiss. She gave a sigh. Slowly, he claimed more and more territory, touching her stomach, her hip, her thigh. He threw his leg over hers and wedged her underneath him. Feeling no sign of protest, he forged ahead.

He pressed his lips to hers then explored the exquisitely soft side of her neck and nibbled her earlobe again. She burst into gooseflesh and arched her back with an involuntary groan. She definitely liked it. Damn, she felt like heaven waiting to happen. The scent in her hair was fresh and fruity and reminded him of pomegranates. He loved the smooth feel of her legs. This woman, oh, this woman was driving him mad.

This isn't fair. You're seducing her when you know she has a date with another man tonight. She deserves better than that. Gavin wanted to beat the tiny voice in the back of his mind sense-less to shut it up. He wanted to unbutton Bethany's blouse and worship her breasts. He wanted to be inside her again, closer than sin. *She deserves better than a quick roll on the couch.*

Damn! Couldn't his conscience just shut up and back off for a few more minutes?

She deserves better. The thoughts ruined his amorous mood. *Damn it all!*

He broke away, but he saw how her eyes were closed, and how she had a look of near ecstasy on her face just from their foreplay. He had done that to her, and he loved the powerful feeling it gave him. He remembered her face when he'd last made love to her, and wanted to see that look again. He was still as hard as granite, but couldn't do anything about it now. He kissed the tip of her nose and she opened her eyes.

"I'd better let you get ready for your date tonight." He glanced at his watch. "You're going to need some time to get rid of my beard burns."

She remained limp and relaxed in his arms. He fought an urge to start kissing her again, especially between that sweet bit of cleavage popping out of her snug top.

"What time is it?" she sighed.

"Almost four."

She shot upright and her head caught his chin. A sharp pain made him grab his jaw and grimace.

"Oh, I'm sorry," she said, rubbing her forehead.

He patted her shoulder and managed a painful smile. "It's OK. Are you all right?"

"I'm fine." She squirmed out of his arms. "You're kidding about the time, right?"

He shook his head, still stroking his face. "Patrick has probably eaten his way through the pizza parlor by now."

She jumped off the couch and gathered up the glasses from the table.

He reluctantly stood and straightened his clothes. "Well, it's been really nice. Especially the last fifteen minutes or so." He laughed at his own audacity. *Get her all lathered up and then split. Good going, Riordan.* Sudden concern about Larry reaping his reward for putting Beth in the mood made him take pause.

Nah. She wasn't like that. He smirked. *Unless it's with me.*

"I hope you have a great time tonight." He headed for the door. "Thanks for coming along to Patrick's game. And don't forget about me later when you're on your hot date with Larry the lab guy."

Beth strode out of the kitchen and approached him with fire in her eyes. She grabbed his sore jaw and planted a rough kiss on his mouth. It hurt, but he liked it.

After she'd lit a firecracker under his shoes, she tore herself away abruptly. "And don't *you* forget about *me* for one second tonight."

CHAPTER SEVEN

"WHY didn't you get an EKG?" Gavin grumbled, and glanced at the clock in his office. It was twelve-fifteen a.m. He redirected a disappointed stare back to his resident. "How hard would it have been to draw cardiac enzymes with the other labs?" He peppered the cherub-faced Jablonsky with indignant blinks and tossed the stack of paperwork back at him. The young doctor squirmed in his chair. "How many hours has the woman been in our emergency department? The least you could have done was get an EKG. You were so focused on a gall-bladder diagnosis that you missed the bigger picture. The fact is, women present with heart disease differently than men. You're a smart guy, you should know that."

Gavin shoved back in his chair and tightened his lips. Maybe he was coming off too harsh. Everyone made mistakes. Jablonsky was no different. But working the ED required a person to keep on his toes, to consider all possibilities, and to rule out things one ailment at a time, like a medical detective. Jablonsky had used poor judgement, and now the patient would have to pay. "You're not a med student any more, Richard—you're a second-year ED resident. Now, go back out there and tell the lady she needs to get stuck by the lab again, and run an EKG."

"Yes, sir. I'll remember that in the future, sir."

"For crying out loud, Richard, this isn't the military. Call me Gavin."

"Yes, si— Gavin." Dismissed, Jablonsky snatched the paperwork up from Gavin's desk and backed out of the office.

Damn. He'd just chewed out one of his best residents. He'd make a point of catching up with him later and apologizing. But right now he had paperwork to complete and Jablonsky had a patient to see to.

Rather than sitting at home alone, knowing Bethany was on a date, Gavin had come to the hospital at around nine to give Maguire a few extra hours off duty with his wife and new baby. Maguire's relief would be in at one, and until then Gavin would catch up with some of the mountain of reports in his in-box. Unable to concentrate, he tossed his pen across the desk and decided not to think about what Beth might or might not be doing on her date. But the suspense was killing him.

He thought about Patrick instead. Now that his son had moved back in with him, whenever Patrick was gone, the house felt too big. And what was it with kids today? Did they all have to spend the night at each other's houses all the time? Patrick was so excited that his new friends had invited him to sleep over and play their newest computer game that Gavin hadn't been able to come up with a good reason to say no. Especially after their recent heart-to-heart talk when Patrick had admitted he didn't think anyone liked him, and how he'd had trouble making friends at his new school.

Carmen appeared at the office door shortly

after the resident left. "Sheesh, Gavin, what have you been saying? Jablonsky's lip was almost quivering." Teasing as usual but unlike her usual perky self, she looked haggard and pale.

"What are you doing here?"

"I picked up a night shift for one of the other nurses. You know my aversion to spending Saturday night alone. I'd much rather work."

She plopped into the chair Jablonsky had just vacated. "Mercy Hospital is my life, Gavin. What else can I say?" she asked rhetorically.

He'd heard it all before. Her husband had divorced her and a few years later both kids had moved out. He knew how hard it was for her— hard enough to keep her working fifty-hour weeks. Maybe that was the same reason he worked as if the end of the world was coming. Loneliness. Well, he didn't feel lonely with his son around…and when he was with Beth.

Carmen crossed her legs and leaned on one hip and elbow. "Maybe I should ask you the same thing. What are you doing here? Didn't you have something going with Miss Allergy today?"

He gave Carmen an irritated glance and mumbled, "She has a date."

"What?" She sat up straighter and her eyes emerged from post-nap status to fully awake.

"What do you know about Larry, the lab guy?"

Carmen sputtered a laugh. "Larry Rossmore, the evening lab supervisor? She's out with Larry? Ha." She worked to put a serious expression back on her face. "I can read the headline now: LUKEWARM LARRY ABSCONDS WITH HOT ER DOC'S MAIN SQUEEZE."

"Keep the commentary to yourself, would you please? Just tell me about the guy." Gavin suppressed a smile, feeling transported back in time to grammar school, pumping a friend for information about his big crush.

She drew in a long breath and searched the floor for her answer. "I guess he's nice enough. Never married. Are you yanking my chain? She actually turned you down for a date with *him*?"

Gavin festered in his chair and defended himself. "Evidently their date was arranged a long time ago. Before we met." He rubbed his still-tender jaw and thought about what they'd been doing on her couch before she'd made him see stars with her surprisingly hard head. "What I don't get is how much the fact that she's out with him is *bugging* me."

A gentle expression lit Carmen's dark eyes. A look Gavin had rarely seen except when she watched Patrick. "You've got it bad." She stood to leave.

"You don't know the half of it." Under different circumstances, maybe he'd tell Carmen the full story. He needed someone to help him figure out how he'd fallen so head over heels for a woman in record time—a woman who happened to be carrying his child, no less. If things could only be perfect, he mused.

He could trust Carmen to keep the news to herself. But she was getting ready to start her shift and he did have that apology to make.

"Cardiac arrest. Room two." Boomed over the intercom.

Gavin recognized the room number as the one in which Jablonsky had been treating gall-bladder symptoms. He jumped up and headed for the door, almost running into a nurse pushing the crash cart toward room two. He took over and rolled the huge red box inside.

"Everyone out of here except the code team," Jablonsky commanded.

Like bumper cars, the EKG technician, rolling the portable electrocardiogram out of the door, almost collided with Gavin. "Have you run a 12-lead?"

"Just now."

Gavin positioned the cart close to the bed. All the emergency equipment they'd need was either on top of or inside the crash cart—everything else was clutter in an already cramped room.

"Stick around," Gavin said to the technician.

A nurse grabbed the backboard from the cart and with the help of Jablonsky placed it under the patient's back. Another nurse grabbed an Ambu-bag and hooked it to the wall. Another broke the lock on the cart and yanked open a drawer.

Jablonsky found an airway and worked to insert it into the patient's throat.

"How long has she been in V-tach?" Gavin asked.

"Just started," Jablonsky replied. Gavin could only imagine the guilt his resident felt, especially after the tongue-lashing Gavin had dished out a few minutes earlier.

Though the heart monitor showed an erratic wide ventricular rhythm, the first nurse still checked the carotid artery for a pulse. The patient needed an electrical jolt to reset her heart, and once it was up and running again they could figure out what type of cardiac damage had occurred. The before-and-after 12-lead EKG would be the key. But not now. Now was life-or-death time. Everyone and everything else had to clear the room.

Gavin ran the code with studied calm. Only a fine tremor betrayed his adrenaline rush. Years of practice had taught him to move slowly and deliberately for the patient's good. Over time he had learned when he allowed himself to get caught up in the frantic battle for life, mistakes happened. Now, at the risk of appearing too casual, he held defibrillator paddles in readiness and called out orders to save the life of a sixty-something grandmother so she could spend another spring with her family.

A few minutes more into the code, after a second zap with the defibrillator, the V-tach stalled, flat-lined and miraculously the first blip of normal sinus rhythm returned.

He'd let an obviously relieved Jablonsky and the rest of the code team take over from here.

Several minutes later, back in his office nursing a weak cup of mint tea, Gavin stroked his jaw. He was tired with just *thinking* about Beth and wanted to see her. Edgy and loaded with pent-up tension, he eyed the phone. One in the morning. Would she be home yet?

Beth lay in bed, staring at the ceiling, trying hard to fall asleep. She'd enjoyed a pleasant evening out, but if she was honest with herself, she'd rather have spent the evening with Gavin. He'd been on her mind all night and it'd kept her feeling restless. They'd had such a great time at the soccer game, and his afternoon kisses had sent fireworks up her spine. If she'd spent the evening with him, by now they might have been wrestling beneath the sheets.

Why did her mind always wind up in the bedroom when she thought about Gavin?

Where he was concerned, she was probably better off playing it safe. Too late! She tugged at her covers in frustration, rolled onto her side and squeezed her eyes closed. If she had to resort to counting sheep, she would. One. Two. Three. Four.

The phone blasted out in the dark, bringing a gut reaction with it—*something's wrong with Mom.* With adrenaline pumping through her, she answered, "Ma?"

"You're home." It was Gavin.

Elated to hear his voice, she didn't disclose her satisfaction. "What makes you think I'm alone?"

The show had been terrific, but the evening with Larry had seemed endless. And she was damned if Gavin hadn't been right! When Larry had walked her to the door, she had looked in her purse to locate her keys, and he'd moved in for a kiss. She'd turned her head fast and his mouth had only caught her cheek.

"Very funny."

Gavin grew quiet for a moment, and took a breath before speaking. "The way I see it, we can do this one of two ways." The hour of the call and the conviction in his voice confirmed his intent. Her skin prickled in anticipation. "I can take an antihistamine and come to your place. Or you can put on something slinky and meet me at mine."

A practical thought popped into her mind. "What about Patrick?"

"He's spending the night with his new friends, which gave me the idea to hold a slumber party of my own."

Gavin wanted to be with her. Wasn't that what she'd just been wishing for? The heady thought of what would soon happen gave her chills, and at the risk of sounding easy she was blunt. "How soon?"

"How about five minutes ago?"

Thirty minutes later she pulled up to Gavin's gate, which immediately opened. He'd been watching and waiting. Something about that gave her another thrill. A tiny fraction of her brain called out, Are you crazy? She ignored it.

She'd never driven anywhere in her nightgown before. Even though she'd covered it with a hooded sweatshirt, there was something daring and exciting about it, which turned her on even more.

She parked and, letting a single kernel of doubt take hold, nervously gathered her makeshift overnight bag. An old canvas tote with the words "Nurses Do It for Love", handed out by Mercy Hospital on Nurse Day a couple years back, held her essential belongings.

She'd had the excuse of peach daiquiri intoxication the last time she'd made love with Gavin. What was her pretext this time? The answer was simple. Stone-cold sober, she wanted him. The rationale she'd used on the drive over had started with the fact that he'd turned out to be an honorable guy when she'd told him she was pregnant, and had offered to help with expenses. It had continued with the memory of their thighs repeatedly brushing in the hot sun all during the soccer game and had ended with the thought of the dynamite kiss he'd stolen from her before he'd left her apartment the previous afternoon. Her body was running on autopilot and logic got forced into the backseat where it would remain until daylight.

The thought of spending the next few hours naked and in bed with Gavin already had her hot and moist.

After tuning out the last whisper of reason, she eased across the driveway and up the porch stairs as if she was a burglar. The cool air tempered the warmth and excitement circulating throughout her body. Maybe she was out of her mind but right now, with her senses heightened and all systems ready to go, she was glad.

Gavin leaned against the doorframe, his dark eyes glinting in the night. He already had his shirt off and his low-slung boxers ready to tug down. Funny how quickly she noticed that. Her heart palpitated at the sight of him. They wouldn't waste time with small talk.

Her breathing went awry.

As she approached, he reached for her bag with

one hand and her elbow with the other, pulling her inside. Only one small nightlight lit the living room, making a dark and intimate cave.

"What took you so long?" He closed the door, tossed her bag on the nearest counter, dug his fingers into her hair and bent to kiss her hello. Sparks flew before she even opened her mouth. The greeting went on for several more delicious mint-flavored kisses. His welcome grew harder and poked against her stomach, sending a deep pulsing message. She let go of every last whimpering and annoying resistance. She'd deal with reality later. *After* they'd made love.

Without further words, he led her down the hall to the bedroom. Excitement coiled tight as she followed.

Candlelight dappled the walls of the bedroom with shape-shifting shadows. She detected the subtle scent of musk and spices. His bedcover had been pulled back, exposing shiny dark-green silk sheets. Exhilarated by the atmosphere, she'd never felt more wanted in her life.

As his sexy bedroom eyes drilled into her, heat

flickered across her chest and rose up her neck. He enveloped her in his arms and backed her up to the bed, where they toppled over.

His hands moved over her, kindling chills and tingles everywhere they touched. He peeled her spaghetti straps off her shoulders and worked the nightgown down her body while she snaked her way out of it. His breathing grew faster and roughened as he savored her inch by inch. Baring all, she stretched and posed like her cat Lila. He gently touched one of her breasts, which tightened and peaked under his attention. With a steamy smile he cupped and lifted her. She answered by pressing against him and prodding with her hips.

In a flash his boxers were gone. For the first time Beth studied him completely naked: long torso, flat abdomen, powerful thighs, and fully erect. His handsomeness took away what was left of her ragged breath.

Their first time together they'd only removed the necessary clothing to do the deed. Tonight they'd have the chance to see, feel and explore each other at their leisure. The heady thought fed her already straining excitement as she reached for him.

He dipped his head and their lips tugged and playfully tore at each other, growing more serious with each kiss. Beth anchored her arms around his neck and rolled on top of Gavin. After a few more kisses he rolled her back where she'd been, beneath him. Preferring the upper hand, she threw her leg over his hip and rolled back yet again, loving the rough and tumble dance. All the while their lips kept contact as she tasted, teased, and discovered a special spot below Gavin's ear that intensified his obvious desire for her. He moaned when she found it. She stroked his chest and discovered his nipples were as erect as hers.

As their bodies melded into each other, she shifted over his skin, inhaling his scent deeply and tucking it into her memory. She rubbed her hands over his shoulders and back, marveling at the strength and power she felt. Gavin pulled her close, mashing himself against her breasts.

Only then did she remember they were tender from her pregnancy.

He pulled back and stroked her stomach, caressing the flesh above her womb then bending to kiss the spot where their deep connection could not be denied. When he lifted his head, their eyes met in silent understanding. A geyser of emotions poured out, mixing with her intense physical desire, almost making her cry.

He balanced on his knuckles, and delved into her eyes with a look so penetrating she surrendered every part of her body to him. She'd hold nothing back. Ready long before she'd reached his house, Beth opened her legs and his steel-strong thigh rolled over hers. With one glance they both realized there was no need to don a condom. Beth cupped his shoulders and Gavin entered her. He made a long steamy hiss as he filled her. Pregnancy heightened her sensitivity. She couldn't breathe, the pleasure was so intense.

He groaned and she rolled with him as they got reacquainted and created their own special rhythm. Heat flamed deep in her center, sparked and spread outward to her stomach. Hot shivers fanned across her breasts, pinching their tips, then escaped up her neck and into her scalp. Her skin almost steamed with heat. She sucked air through her teeth and arched, aware of every point of sensation.

Growing even firmer, Gavin probed and rocked her into taking him deeper inside. The rush was so consuming she made a guttural sound, pulling him closer and deeper still. He thrust faster and she cried out, quickly quieting herself down, but he continued his rhythm and she erupted with feelings so intense she couldn't bite back the sounds. She'd never made a sound with her ex-husband.

In full stride, he took her, for what seemed like for ever, and finally drove her to the edge as she crested into blissful release. Delicious spasms burrowed and throbbed into her very center, making her groan and buck against them.

He echoed her pleasure and moved faster and harder. She wasn't sure she could take any more but didn't want him to stop. Wave after exquisite wave began at the soles of her feet and spiraled upward, circling her skin like a swarm of electric fireflies. Gavin stiffened and surged powerfully, bringing her quickly to a second climax when he came.

She lingered outside time, paralyzed with pleasure, unable to string a single coherent thought together. Leftover tingles and throbs traveled deliciously throughout her body. He'd brought her to the brink of heaven.

A moment later he collapsed next to her, kissed her chin and gruffly whispered, "We've definitely got something going on."

Beth grinned at the understatement, but was too spent to utter a sound. Instead, she curled her arm around his neck and kissed him back.

Gavin rose early, took a quick shower and strode to the kitchen to make a pot of decaf for Bethany and whip up his banana oatmeal pancakes. He only made them for special people. Patrick would be jealous he'd missed out, but Gavin would be sure to save some for him to heat up and eat later.

Today, his usual edgy attitude had been replaced with an optimistic "all is right with the world" mellow feeling. He grinned at his cup of coffee. Great sex was life's best tranquilizer. And being more than sufficiently immunized, on his first Sunday off in three weeks, he'd simply enjoy whatever the day brought his way.

He sipped his coffee and glanced out the kitchen window, noticing the recent blooms on the vine around his veranda. Morning glory purple. Beautiful. Unable to fool himself any longer, he admitted it wasn't just fantastic sex where Beth was concerned. He'd let himself fall for her. After his divorce, he'd promised to never let it happen again. He smiled at the thought of Bethany and all she had to offer. She even came complete with a ready-made family. Was he ready to deal with that?

At least he'd held off from getting involved for over three years. Being honest, the thought of marrying again made his toes turn to ice. Keeping it real, he had a way to go before he'd be ready to make a huge step like that, even though Beth was already pregnant. And he'd have to tell Patrick about her sooner or later. It may as well be today when he came home.

Oh! Patrick! Gavin looked at the clock.

His head bobbed up in time to see Patrick and his two newest friends walking up the steps to the front door, a few minutes earlier than scheduled. He must have used his own key to open the gate. The boy noticed him through the window and casually waved. Gavin could read his lips. "Hi, Dad."

He rushed to the front door to let them in.

"Hey!" He bent down and hugged him. "You're home bright and early."

"Yeah!" Patrick broke free from his hug. "I want to show them something in my room."

"OK. Hi, guys. Did you have fun last night?"

All three boys called out in unison, "Yeah," as they rushed down the hall.

Gavin grabbed Beth's bag from the counter and skidded down the corridor in his socks. He careened off the walls and hurled into his room. Bethany lay naked in a pool of sheets, her hair covering her face. She looked so cute he wanted to climb back in bed with her but, under the circumstances, couldn't give it a second thought.

"Beth," he whispered hoarsely. "Wake up. Patrick's home. Put on some clothes. Quick."

She rose up and gaped at him. "Patrick's home?"

He rushed around the bed as she slowly came to, and rummaged through her tote, finding a T-shirt and some shorts. He tossed them at her. "Here, put these on."

She grabbed the clothes and scampered toward the master bathroom.

He watched with great admiration as her curvy hips jogged away. But Patrick's presence worked better than any cold shower.

To his dismay, he heard faucets being turned on. *No. We don't have time.* But he couldn't very well deny the mother of his future baby a shower, could he?

He heard the boys run back down the hall and Patrick's door slam. Gavin followed them back to the kitchen. Matt and Chad said goodbye and trotted off.

"I'll see you at school tomorrow," Patrick said, excitedly waving goodbye.

"OK," the boys replied, and disappeared down the steps to the front gate.

Gavin followed them to thank their parents for having Patrick over.

What would Patrick think when he saw Bethany at their house so early this morning?

Hey, guess what? Bethany and I went for a run this morning, and I was just making banana oatmeal pancakes while she showers.

Nah, he couldn't lie to his son. When he returned to the kitchen, Patrick was sitting at the counter, stirring the dry ingredients for the pancake batter.

"Guess who came to visit?" Gavin said.

"Mom?"

Predictable. Why had he baited the boy with such a stupid question? He hoped he wouldn't be disappointed. "No. Bethany."

Patrick's eyes lit up, surprising Gavin. "Where is she?"

Don't lie. Just don't tell him everything. He cleared his throat. "She needed to take a shower."

"Oh." He continued to stir the flour mixture.

Gavin watched for a glimmer of understanding, but didn't see a light bulb go off behind Patrick's innocent nine-year-old gaze. How soon, with puberty just over the horizon, would that change?

"Why didn't you call me before you came home early?" Gavin asked, measuring out the milk.

"I knew you'd be here, Dad."

Gavin savored the confidence coming from his son, but what if he'd spent the night at Bethany's? "What if I'd gotten called in on an emergency?"

"I guess I didn't think about that."

"Next time you should call home first."

"OK." Patrick made another stir and soon lost interest. "Call me when breakfast is ready," he said, as he wandered back down the hall.

Beth emerged from Gavin's bedroom and heard a peculiar spraying sound from behind Patrick's door. She tipped her head and stood in the hall, listening. He coughed quietly.

The handle on the door twisted and Patrick peeked out.

"What's going on?" she asked, with concern and a touch of curiosity.

He started, eyes wide, mouth open. "Nothing."

A distinct disinfectant smell wafted outside. "What are you spraying in there?"

He coughed again. "Just some air freshener."

"Are you cleaning your room?"

"Yeah."

"Let me see what a good job you've done."

As if it were possible, his eyes got wider. He froze.

Even more curious, Beth pushed on the door and, looking very unhappy, Patrick stepped back.

His room was a typical little-boy mess, with piles of dirty clothes left right where they'd come off, toys strewn across the floor, bed unmade. The air freshener sat on his bedside table—Spring Garden Scent. She couldn't help but tease him. "Yeah, I can see how hard you've been working."

She noticed his closet door was ajar and walked toward it. Patrick rushed ahead of her and shut it.

Her antennae went up. "You're hiding something, aren't you?"

"No." He leaned against the door.

"You're acting awfully suspicious for someone who isn't hiding anything."

He folded his arms and jutted out his chin. She tried another tack. "I just thought I heard something in your room. With it kind of messy like this, you don't have rats do you?" Her attempt to tease fell flat. Patrick looked mortified. "I don't mean to say you've got rats roaming around in your room, Patrick. It's just that I thought I heard a strange squeaky-wheel kind of sound. It's hard to explain, but it seems to be coming from…" She pointed to his closet. Hoping to coax him into confiding in her, she continued, "Have you got any idea what it could be?"

He stared at his toes for a few seconds. "Will you promise not to tell my dad?"

CHAPTER EIGHT

PATRICK opened the closet door, switched on the light, and showed Beth two makeshift cages at the back of the walk-in wardrobe. They were complete with spinning wheels, food dispensers and water troughs. Two round fur balls stirred from their separate ceramic sleeping caves and began wiggling their noses and whiskers as they padded through the shredded cedar to check things out.

Beth tried not to smile. "Honey, I can't keep secrets from your dad, and you shouldn't either. But I will promise to help you out."

He sighed and twisted up his mouth. "Dad won't let me keep Muffy and Puff if he finds out."

"How long have you had hamsters?"

"I've had Muffy ever since I moved in with Dad."

"And what about Puff?"

"I snuck her home that time from my friend Bobby's when I went for the weekend in Irvine. His mom didn't know he had one either, it was our secret, but he got scared and asked me to take Puff home."

"How did you do that?"

"In my backpack. They're real quiet."

How could a nine-year-old boy manage to keep such a secret from his father for almost two months? Surely the housekeeper knew about the secret pets?

"Why haven't you told your father, Patrick?"

"He's allergic to cats because they have fur, and my hamsters have fur." Tears welled in his eyes, and his chin quivered. "Bobby is my best friend. He gave Muffy to me. It was our best-friend secret. I couldn't tell."

"Your asthma has been worse since you moved in with your dad. You tested borderline positive for cats. Maybe you're allergic to hamsters."

"No. I can't be. I love them." He picked them

up, one in each hand, and rubbed them against his cheeks. He giggled when one got loose and crawled across his shoulders and on top of his head. He produced a clear plastic sphere the size of a basketball. "Bobby gave this to me, too." He opened it and dropped the other hamster inside then sealed it back up. "That's how I brought Puff home in my backpack. See? It even has air holes. They can roll around my room and see everything from in there."

Beth shook her head and smiled. Her heart ached for the boy who'd had his world disrupted first by his parents' divorce then by his mother leaving for England on a sudden whim. The boy who'd lost a cat because his father might have been allergic to it and his mother hadn't wanted to keep it. Could she blame Patrick for hiding his favorite pets?

It made sense he'd want to keep something special from his best friend if he'd had to move away. But the burden of keeping such a secret must have weighed heavily on him for the past two months. Was Gavin so distracted with work that he'd never discovered two hamsters living in his son's closet?

The hamster rolled around the room, bumping into piles of clothes and furniture, looking curious and as cute as could be. Beth couldn't help but grin. Patrick put the other hamster, a much smaller one, into his baggy cargo shorts pocket. "I'm not allergic. I never wheeze when I'm around them."

"But you were coughing before you opened the door. And I've noticed lots of times that when you first come out of your room you cough. And yesterday you were wheezing."

"The air freshener tickles my throat. That's all."

As an allergy nurse, Beth knew there were both allergies and irritants in the world. Cigarette smoke and perfume were irritants. Pollens and dander were allergens. Each could set off wheezing. And aerosol spray with a sharp fragrance could definitely irritate someone's lungs, even if they didn't have asthma. Though she hadn't tested Patrick for a hamster allergy, it would be simple enough, if it meant easing his mind. She could test Gavin, too.

"If the air freshener bothers your asthma, why use it?"

"'Cos Dad's allergic to it. I want to clean the air."

Little-boy logic touched her softest spot. She bent down on her knees and looked into Patrick's gray eyes. "Oh, honey, that's so sweet." She didn't have the heart to explain to him that if his dad was allergic to hamsters, all the air freshener in the world wouldn't help. "May I hold him?"

Patrick took the second hamster from his pocket and placed him in her cupped hands. All fur, he hardly weighed anything. She giggled at the feel of his tiny paws on her palms. There had to be a way to work things out so Patrick could keep his special pets. Needing time to think things through, she rubbed Puff against her chin. "You are so cute."

"Breakfast!" Gavin's rich baritone nearly shook the walls.

Patrick tossed Bethany a questioning look. How the heck was she supposed to handle this? She wanted to develop trust with Patrick, but she didn't want to betray Gavin. The best thing to do was to let them work out their own problems. "Promise me you'll tell your dad."

The look of relief on the boy's face made her smile. "I promise."

"Soon," she reinforced.

"The pancakes are getting cold, you guys," Gavin called from the kitchen.

"OK," Patrick agreed.

They carefully closed the door and washed their hands, then rushed down the hall to the kitchen to eat.

During breakfast, Gavin said, "I've been thinking. What we need is more one-on-one time, Patrick. You know, just us guys."

"Yeah!" Beth almost laughed at the transition in Patrick's mood from secretive to exuberant.

"Don't you have a free week coming up at school? Why don't the two of us go to Mammoth in a couple of weeks for the opening of the trout season?"

Patrick cheered. "Cool!"

Beth felt like a voyeur watching a happy family scene play out. Where did she belong in the picture? With all of the making up for lost time needed between father and son, maybe there wasn't room for her in Gavin's life right now. She'd promised to be honest with herself this time around, and admitted it hurt, but tried her best to cover up for Gavin and Patrick's sakes. "That sounds like a great plan."

Gavin's pleased gaze lingered. He gave Beth a serene smile, reached across the table and squeezed her arm. A special softness colored his eyes with a hint of something else. Passion? Lust? Caution?

She'd given herself completely to him last night. Couldn't he feel it? And if he did, had it made any difference to him at all? She'd chastised Patrick for keeping secrets from Gavin, but right now she was harboring a huge revelation of her own. She'd fallen for Gavin in a big way.

On Monday morning Gavin showed up bright and early in the allergy department to start his shots. Beth marveled over the giddy reaction he always managed to pull out of her. After test-dosing him for grass, trees, and weed mix, plus cat, two on each arm, and surreptitiously throwing in a skin test for hamster, he rolled down his sleeves.

They smiled at each other, and his smile quickly escalated to steamy. With his sensual full lips and the cleft in his chin, how could it not? The fire in his eyes made her cheeks flame. He leaned in and said under his breath, "I missed you last night."

Heat pulsed through her against her will. She blinked and cleared her throat to gather her composure. Her entire head felt as if it was glowing hot. She was at work—she couldn't let the other patients in the waiting room see that she and Gavin were more than friends. Or, worse, see her melt into a puddle at his feet. "We should probably talk about that." She softened her voice. "It was a close call with Patrick coming home so early."

Gavin rubbed the back of his neck and exhaled. A million thoughts seemed to be running through his mind, but he didn't utter another sound. She'd added a huge load to his existing burdens by being pregnant.

Finally, he spoke. "We'll have to be more careful next time."

At least he was talking about a next time. She kept her profound relief under wraps. Snapping back into professional mode, she said, "I've got more shots to give. Take a seat and I'll call you in thirty minutes to check your arms for reactions."

"I love it when you get bossy," he said, before he strolled away.

Beth put extra effort into concentrating on her patient lineup instead of how gorgeous Gavin looked in his tailored gray slacks and butter-cream-yellow shirt. He seemed intent on reading the business section of the newspaper, but occasionally she caught him watching her from the corner of his eye as she worked. Whenever their gazes met, heat waves rolled across her skin.

Grateful for a week busy with extra jobs and assorted other plans with Jillian and her mother—like finally telling her about her pregnancy—she'd do her best to keep him out of her mind.

Finally, his thirty minutes were up and though she was relieved to see he wasn't allergic to hamsters, she was surprised at how much the weed shot festered on his arm. "We should dilute the serum and start you at an even lower dose when you get your next injections."

"Whatever you say. You're the allergy guru."

She folded her arms. "And I won't give you your shots next time if you don't show me your EpiPen," she said with firm resolve.

"You know how that turns me on, right?"

He pushed away from the podium, stopped in his tracks, then turned and gave her his special smile, showing charm enough to knock the stethoscope right off her shoulders. So much for resolve.

Not thinking about Gavin Riordan for the rest of the day would take every last bit of her rapidly depleting energy.

Between Beth's busy schedule and Gavin's weekend emergency department demands, they didn't have a chance to spend any time together the rest of the week. He'd been grateful when she'd offered to take Patrick to the latest animated movie on Sunday afternoon, and that evening they agreed to meet up for dinner. Seeing her less than one week later, Gavin could have sworn Bethany's breasts had gotten even bigger than he'd remembered.

She wore a loose tunic-style top, but nothing could hide the increased size of her chest. She radiated beauty and it took all of his strength to resist pulling her into his arms and telling her exactly what was on his mind.

They worked in the kitchen, side by side, preparing Patrick's favorite meal, spaghetti. Even Patrick got in on the act, thanks to Bethany's quick thinking.

"Wash your hands then tear this lettuce into this bowl. When you're done, I'll help you chop cucumber and tomato."

Gavin smiled, seeing his son's face brighten when he asked, "Can I hold the knife?"

"We can hold it together at first, then, when you've got the hang of it, I'll watch and see how you do."

"Cool!"

Gavin stood close enough to Beth to notice her

faint perfume. He wanted to do so much more than that, like nuzzle her neck and inhale the scent of her hair. He wanted to taste her lips and caress her soft skin, too, but that would have to wait for another time.

Bright-eyed Patrick appeared to be just as infatuated, which posed a special problem if things didn't work out. In a certain way Patrick was dating Bethany, too. And Gavin couldn't bear to be responsible for Patrick getting his heart broken. His mother had hurt him enough by taking off for four months out of the blue. Did Patrick really need another woman to win him over, get his hopes up, then potentially let him down?

Gavin scratched his chin. Even the simple act of dating got complicated when kids were involved. Not to mention the baby on the way.

Even if things didn't work out between him and Beth, he'd make sure Patrick knew and got involved with his half-sibling. Both children deserved nothing less.

A nagging reminder that he'd short-changed his son on so many levels was the only thing holding Gavin back where Beth was concerned. Every time he wanted to move forward with her, guilt—like a slip knot—pulled him back. He'd purposely stayed away all week. How could he juggle his new relationship with his son and bring Bethany into his life at the same time?

Watching them chop the vegetables made him long for the possibility of much more. Dared he dream that everyone could be happy? It was obvious they liked each other. Beth had great mothering skills, which seemed to come naturally, and Patrick responded to her beautifully. But was she the "one"? Before he'd consider marriage again, he'd have to be positive. If that was even possible, or did falling in love always require a leap of faith?

Beth made her own garlic butter concoction for the bread, and she let Patrick spread it on before popping the bread into the oven to brown it. Being around her pulled on his heart more and more, awakening a whole new set of feelings he'd kept packed away since his divorce. Thoughts about being in love again, sharing his life with a partner, possibly being a blended family, kept pushing their way into his mind. With his new-found love of parenting and another child on the way, a kick of anxiety kept him edgy and worried he wouldn't be able to pull any of it off. And one divorce per lifetime was more than enough.

After he'd poured the boiling water and cooked noodles into the colander, Bethany ladled on the sauce and they each carried their own bowl to the table. Gavin couldn't remember the last time he'd had a family dinner in his home, but he liked the way it felt. By the look on Patrick's face, he did, too. Gavin had hated being an only child being raised by his grandmother, having quiet, sedate meals. Patrick would probably love to have a brother or sister.

Bethany ate with gusto, which was a change from a few weeks earlier. Patrick tried to impress her with his ear-twisting, noodle-sucking trick. She laughed and gave it a try, getting spaghetti sauce all over her cheeks. Gavin wanted to clean her up with kisses. Instead, he gave his best shot at repeating the silly stunt. Seeing his two favorite people enjoying their meal made Gavin swear he'd never tasted better sauce in his life. This was a dinner he promised to never forget, and hoped to repeat for many years to come.

But what about Beth? How could he give her what she needed—no, deserved—while being true to his promise to his son to be there for him, no matter what? Would Patrick feel cheated if he pursued a relationship with Beth? The questions blurred his concentration and made his head throb and, worse yet, made him lose his appetite. What should have been an enjoyable meal wound up churning in his stomach.

Later, after a heated game of Scrabble, he kissed Beth goodnight on the doorstep and fought an immediate desire for more.

They grinned at each other and he saw the flare of passion in her eyes. God, he wanted to pull her back inside, but every thought he'd been turning over in his mind crowded out the invitation.

Knowing it was cowardly, but needing some time and space to figure things out, he decided not to see Bethany again until her next obstetrics appointment when Karen Scott would do an ultrasound. And that decision proved to keep him awake and lonely most of the night.

A flight of butterflies fluttered in Gavin's stomach at the thought of seeing what was going on in Beth's womb. There was nothing like a black and white picture to make it real. He fondly remembered seeing Patrick at his first ultrasound ten years ago, the size of a mere lima bean. The thought made him smile. Soon he and Bethany would have to go public with their involvement, and from there there'd be no turning back.

That was one of the reasons he'd planned the fishing trip with Patrick. They'd take off on Friday afternoon, as soon as Patrick got out of school, drive to Bishop, spend the night at the motel that served warm cookies each afternoon, then head on to Mammoth on Saturday morning. When the time was right, he'd ask Patrick what he thought about his dad being with Beth.

Afterwards, he'd come home renewed and

ready to tackle the reality of being a father a second time. He just needed this last bit of time alone with his son to pave the way.

He tapped on the examination door of Karen's obstetrics and gynecology suite. A muffled voice answered, telling him to come inside. Beth lay on the stainless-steel exam table covered in white sheets. Her hazel eyes shining, she smiled at him and he strode the three steps across the cramped room to greet her. Her honey-colored hair, pulled back with a band, made her look like a teenager, and a soft rose color glistened on her lips. He wanted to kiss her but refrained. Instead, he took her hand in his. Her fingers were icy cold and he massaged them to warm her up. The poor thing was nervous, and with her history he understood why.

Gavin greeted his colleague by her first name. Karen sat gloved and poised with an ultrasound transducer in one hand and a large tube of lubricant in the other. "Are we ready?"

"Yes, please," Bethany said.

Gavin felt willing, though not quite ready for what was about to happen.

"My bladder is ready to pop," Bethany said.

Karen grinned and squirted a huge glob of gel onto Bethany's lower abdomen. She let out a controlled squeal and squeezed his hand tighter. He wanted to kiss her forehead and tell her how much she meant to him, but didn't say a word in front of Karen.

Karen spoke to Gavin, filling him in on things he presumed she'd already discussed with Bethany. "At Beth's last visit, her fundal height was higher than I'd expect for her EDC."

"EDC?" It had been years since he'd done his obstetrics rotation.

"Estimated date of confinement."

"Ah." Her due date. "It's been a while since I went through this." He squeezed Bethany's fingers. She gripped back and grinned. God, he loved her grin.

Karen continued, "I wanted to confirm her EDC and locate the placenta, as she's had two miscarriages in the past."

The miscarriages. Dear God, Bethany. He squeezed her hand and glanced into her pained gaze. Thinking of their child, and how it would rip his heart out if she miscarried, Gavin's stomach lurched for her losses.

No longer caring what Karen thought, he leaned over and kissed Bethany lightly. "We won't let it happen again," he said, and worried he'd made a promise he couldn't possibly keep the moment he'd said it. But seeing how it had made her smile, he wouldn't have taken it back, even if he could.

The doctor placed the wand-like transducer on Beth's abdomen, pressed and swirled it back and forth as a triangular picture appeared on the bedside screen. She concentrated and brushed the device back and forth over the skin and uterus bouncing sonar waves off the tissue, until she spotted what she was looking for—the gestational sac and a peanut-sized embryo.

"There we go. That little pulsing you see is the heartbeat."

Gavin's mouth dropped open with awe, and Bethany took a quick breath. His heart squeezed at the sight of the fragile life before him. He stole a glance at Beth's face, where he saw love and hope as she watched the ultrasound monitor. He stared back at the screen in wonder, feeling chills, and held Bethany's hand a little too tightly.

Karen used a foot pedal to capture the view for film then before he was ready for her to move on, she pushed the wand at another angle. "Hmm," she said, as she repositioned the device. "Ah, that's what I'm looking for."

She was searching for something other than the baby? The gestational sac and embryo reappeared. Gavin figured it was from a different angle. He grinned again and continued to stare in amazement.

Karen captured another picture and gave a mischievous smile. "I thought you were growing too fast, Beth. You two are the proud parents of twins."

Dazed, Gavin dropped Beth's hand. She rose up onto her elbows and stared skeptically at the monitor. His knees almost buckled. He stepped back. Twins? He followed Bethany's lead and bent forward, studying the screen for every detail he could decipher. Surely this couldn't be true. He'd only just prepared for one more child, and had convinced himself they could work it out—but two?

Karen did a quick maneuver with the wand and reverted back to the first embryo, then back to the other. "See? There are two of them. Two sacs. Two babies. Two placentas. Fraternal twins."

They both instantaneously turned their heads and stared at each other. Bethany's face was easier to read than a book with large print. Shock. Disbelief. Panic? He probably looked the exact same way, because that sure as hell was how he felt.

"Twins?" Bethany croaked.

Gavin broke out in beads of sweat across his forehead. His lungs clamped down to where it was almost difficult to breathe. He said, "Twins?" Feeling as though he was having an out-of-body experience, he searched for a place to sit. There wasn't one.

"Yes. Congratulations. You're having twins." Karen turned off the ultrasound machine and wiped the gel from Bethany's stomach. When she was done, she glanced back and forth between them with a knowing, empathetic look. "It's often a huge surprise to discover you're having twice as many babies as you'd planned."

In their case they hadn't planned for a baby at all! Still stunned, neither of them answered.

"I'll leave you two alone so you can talk."

Before Gavin could reclaim command of his lower jaw and shut his mouth, Karen breezed out of the room and closed the door. He tried to swallow but his throat suddenly felt like a desert. He scrubbed his chin. Surely others had dealt with the same circumstances. There was always room enough in the heart of a family for another child.

He'd let his thoughts take over his face. When he glanced Beth's way, he realized she'd been watching him and had seen his major doubt. Not to mention the lack of celebration at the latest news from their one-night stand. And, worse, she'd seen the fear and insecurity he felt down to his bones.

Desperately needing her to understand he wouldn't run away from his responsibility, he reached for her hand again. It felt limp. Her earlier expression of love and hope had disappeared, and in its place he saw guarded withdrawal.

"I'm really happy about this, Bethany. The more, the merrier. Honestly." Why did it sound so unconvincing?

She shook her head and burst into tears. He enveloped her and hugged her tight while she sobbed. Trying his best to make sense out of her tears, he thought, OK, so there are two babies. Maybe she feels outnumbered. If only he could read her mind.

"Sweetheart, everything will be OK. We'll work things out."

She swiped at her tears and used the sheet to wipe her nose, trying hard to stop crying. "I know," she whimpered. "I just need some time to think about this. Alone."

At a loss for what else to say, he mumbled, "If you want, I'll wait outside while you get dressed."

"That's OK. I know you're busy. You don't have to wait around," she said, obviously trying to regain her composure. "I've got to get back on the job anyway."

Feeling rotten about leaving her, even though she had requested it, he said, "Right. I do, too." Then, experiencing an uncomfortable sense of being shut out, he pecked her on the cheek. "We'll talk about this more later. I'll call you."

Beth was determined not to let history repeat itself. If she hadn't figured it out before, the look on Gavin's face at the news of twins had driven her worst fears home. She'd seen the same look in Neal's eyes when she'd told him about her second pregnancy. Even though she'd allowed herself to fall in love, she couldn't risk her heart on Gavin. The only person in the world she could depend on was herself.

Alone in Dr Scott's exam room, she shrugged off the gown. They'd both been shocked about the twins—she'd cut him some slack there. But beyond shock, she'd read horror in his eyes. He bore the look of a trapped man watching the gate close...and lock. She'd had an insecure sense that he'd been avoiding her all that week. Maybe it hadn't been so far-fetched. As of tomorrow, he'd be out of town with Patrick for a week.

How stupid of her to think that a relationship started in a dark hallway at a party could ever have worked out. The reality of their true circumstances stuck in her throat. Her mouth watered and she started crying again.

Maybe it was the pregnancy hormones, or she was just being a glass-half-empty kind of woman, but she had a terrible feeling about what was to come. Gavin might get overwhelmed by all of the added responsibility and back off from any relationship. News of having twins may have disrupted her life, but she had to admit that she'd disrupted Gavin and Patrick's lives, too. If he dreamed of getting custody of his son back, how would it look in court to admit he'd soon be the father of twins with a woman he wasn't married to?

She used the bathroom.

Now physically relieved, but with her worst fears still growing, she shook her head and buttoned her blouse. Giving a deep sigh, she accepted the inevitable—she'd be going through this pregnancy alone.

Oh, God, how would she handle twins? She'd convinced herself she could pull off single parenting with one baby, but two? How in the world would she do that?

The thought of diapers for two, breastfeeding two, getting one settled before the other needed attention, and two sets of lungs screaming at the same time gave her palpitations.

Neal had always made it clear that his career as a singer had come before their marriage. She had been young and dumb and had settled for it then. But now she'd matured and learned she deserved more than a runner-up spot in anyone's life. Well, it was time to make her stand. If Gavin wasn't on board one hundred percent, she wouldn't wait around for him to catch up. And one thing was more certain than even the twins— she couldn't make him love her.

Once dressed, she left the room, thanked the nurse then headed for the elevator. Beth knew what she had to do. She'd have to start training

Jillian and her mother as future nannies right away. Another possibility popped into her mind, but it could wait. She needed more time to think things through. First she needed to tell her mother she was going to be a grandmother.

Twice.

CHAPTER NINE

GAVIN had phoned, as he'd promised, but Beth had been in the middle of telling her mother about the twins and had let the mobile call go to voice mail. When she played his message later, he'd promised to be in touch when he got back from the fishing trip.

After Neal, Beth had vowed never to let anyone walk all over her again. Even though Gavin had agreed to help out, she couldn't buy diapers and baby food with promises. And the bottom line was that the welfare of her babies could not depend on whether or not Gavin *might* fall in love with her. She would never again put her heart in the hands of someone who didn't know what he wanted.

Beth slept fitfully that night, waking up often. Once awake, her mind replayed the scene with her mother earlier that day. She had feared the poor woman had had a stroke when she'd gone statue still after Beth had shared her news. With Ruth's face etched in shock, it had been several seconds before she'd flushed and fanned herself, while repeating over and over, "Twins?"

Eventually, sheer exhaustion drove Beth to sleep.

The ringing of the phone hurled her from a dream. She lifted her head from the pillow, adrenaline making her jittery, and looked at the clock. Two a.m. The phone rang again.

She fumbled for the receiver. "Hello?"

"A pipe must have burst," Ruth's tense voice cut through the line. "The bathroom and hall are flooded."

Beth bolted upright. "I'll be right over, Mom."

It only took her five minutes once she was at her mother's house to discover what the source of the "burst" pipe was. Ruth had left the stopper in the sink and the ancient faucet had leaked for hours. The stream of water from the overflowing basin had slowly forged a path into the hall. When Ruth had gotten up for a bathroom visit, she'd stepped into a puddle and panicked.

Thank God she hadn't slipped and fallen.

"Mom, there is so much hard water build-up on these old fixtures, it's just about impossible to turn them tight enough to shut them off." Beth mopped the hair away from her face and paddled back toward her mother.

"Well, how am I supposed to know that?" Worry wrote extra lines on her face. "Your father used to take care of this sort of thing."

"I know. This old house is a big responsibility. Why do you think I keep telling you about the senior apartments?" Beth threw an armload of towels onto the ancient wooden floors and used her foot to mop them around the hallway, but got tangled up. Arms flailing, she almost landed on the floor, recovering just in time.

"Oh!" Ruth lunged after her and fell. "Ouch!"

"Mom! Are you OK?"

"I'm fine." But she wasn't fine. She burst into tears. "Are you sure you're pregnant again?"

"Yes," Beth replied, feeling a sudden urge to cry. "I've seen the twins with my own eyes."

She reached out to help pull her mother to her feet.

Beth wondered whether Ruth had been taking her calcium tablets. All she'd need was for her mother to fracture her tailbone or, worse, break her hip.

What would be the best for all of them—Ruth, herself and the twins? Ruth avoided the topic of senior housing as if it were a prison sentence. Beth needed to get her finances under control and her rent was high. The twins needed a family.

"I've been thinking," Beth said, trying to catch her breath. "Why don't I give up my apartment and move back here with you? There's plenty of room for you, me, and the babies."

It *would* help her save money.

Ruth clapped her hands together. "That would be wonderful!" She hadn't looked that ecstatic since the day Beth had graduated from nursing school.

A few hours later, after cleaning and mopping with her mother, Beth crawled back into her own bed, having made the final plans for her decision, wishing she was half as happy as Ruth.

Gavin and Patrick had had enough fishing, but agreed to stay one more night on Thursday. They'd caught their five-trout limit for yet another day. While sitting in their rented boat on June Lake, the only sound water lapping the metal frame, Patrick opened up. "Dad?"

Gavin sat mesmerized by the vast and beautiful lake and the peaceful hush. "Hmm?"

"I think I want to live with you from now on."

"Are you sure?"

Patrick nodded.

Buoyed up with the thought of having his son full time, Gavin grinned. "I'd love that, too, but what about your mother?"

"I love Mom, but…um…I like it with you lots more."

The freckles on Patrick's nose crinkled with his smile when Gavin reached over and gave him a one-armed hug.

He'd have to run Patrick's request by Maureen.

Seeing that she'd discovered a sudden desire to travel the globe and study art history, it wasn't such a bad idea all round. More importantly, he loved Patrick and wanted to see him every day. He may have missed out on living with him through some of his formative years, but he sure as hell didn't want to miss the rest. They liked living together and got along well, and Maureen may have made the biggest mistake of her life by taking off for England this spring. Gavin, having recently been enlightened, would just as soon never go back to the way things had been.

Later, when Patrick had finished a peanut-butter sandwich, he surprised Gavin even more when he broached the subject of Beth. "Maybe Beth could live with us, too."

"You like her that much?" Pleased warmth settled in Gavin's chest.

"Yeah."

"Me, too." He'd given Beth nothing but mixed messages from the start. At first he'd thought his pursuit of her had been merely physical attraction, but when he'd gotten to know her better, he'd realized what a fantastic person she was and how much she could add to his life. Yet he'd pushed her away by avoiding her out of fear of repeating his failure with Maureen.

How could he have let her down more at the ultrasound? He had actually been relieved when she'd told him to go back to work. Coward. How could the poor woman trust him to be there if he took off fishing any time there was a major event? It looked like he had his work cut out to convince Beth he was the kind of guy to trust, who *would* stick around. But he would.

"Hey, Patrick?"

The boy looked from under his fishing cap, his eyes wide and trusting.

"What would you think about having a little brother or sister…or both?"

"I dunno. Babies are kind of boring."

Gavin smiled to himself. Well, they'd soon find out and, whatever it took, he'd help Patrick adjust. Like most things in life, they'd take it one step at a time, and today was definitely a start.

He'd done some major soul-searching while

waiting for the trout to bite all week. He'd met Bethany at this particular time in his life for a purpose. He wouldn't go so far as to call it fate, because the timing couldn't have been worse, and the circumstances couldn't have been more complicated, and he imagined fate to be ideal in all ways. Yet he couldn't deny that all the perfect ingredients for a true romance had been present from the start—chemistry, compatibility, caring. Had he mentioned chemistry?

Now, with Patrick's enthusiastic nod of approval, Gavin could no longer deny all the signs that stared him in the face. He was finally ready to take his relationship with Bethany to the next level, and for the first time since his divorce he would take a leap of faith toward love.

And the thought still scared the hell out of him.

CHAPTER TEN

MONDAY afternoon, Beth took a late lunch. Even though it was dry and windy out, she sat outside on a bench and ate under a Chinese elm tree. She needed time to regroup.

Staying at her mother's all weekend, working in the teen clinic on Friday night and at the soup kitchen on Saturday evening, Beth had dodged Gavin, and had conveniently left her cellphone at home. Today she'd purposely gone to lunch at this time to avoid his scheduled allergy shots. The other nurse could take care of him…if he showed up.

Eating for three was an amazing experience, and she slurped the last of her Tuscan cantaloupe with gusto, wishing she'd brought a few more slices. While wiping her mouth, she checked her watch. It was time to get back to work.

Another gust of wind hit her solidly in the face as she walked toward the clinic building. She pulled her hair back from her eyes, remembering how so many of the ragweed patients had been reacting to their weed shots today. It made sense, with heavy pollen blowing in from the nearby hills. Even though she'd written Gavin out of her life, she couldn't keep him out of her mind for more than minutes at a time. She hoped he had the good sense to take an antihistamine before his shots. And had he ever picked up his EpiPen?

She'd been using the stairs at work, telling herself the exercise was a good thing, but all the while she knew she had the ulterior motive of avoiding Gavin in the elevators.

Two flights up, she heard a door open on the landing above. She turned the corner and glanced up in time to see Gavin heading down.

Oh, God. Her knees wobbled. Had he taken the stairs to avoid her, too?

Her hand trembled on the railing and her mind went fuzzy.

He stopped in his tracks, masking a guarded expression, making it impossible to read him. He stared into her eyes—waiting.

Beth had promised herself that the next time she saw him she'd break things off, and had purposely put it off. Well, here he was.

She thought her heart might explode.

Keep it casual. Don't burn any more bridges. He'll need to be a part of the babies' lives whether we're together or not.

"Hi," she said.

He nodded, with a cautious expression. "Hi."

"Just get your shots?" Her voice wavered in a sorry attempt to sound nonchalant.

He scratched one arm with a vengeance. "Yeah. This one itches like a bee sting."

"I bet it's the weed mix. You shouldn't scratch it. It will just make it worse."

He clenched his jaw.

Enough with the small talk. If life had taught her nothing else, she'd learned to seize an opportunity when it presented itself. She'd promised herself to make a stand, and Gavin was here.

"How was the fishing trip?"

"Really good. There are a few things I'd like to talk to you about, but the hospital stairwell isn't the right place," he said.

Already winded from the steps, knowing what she had to do took the rest of her breath away.

"So, can I see you tonight? Patrick has tai kwon do."

"I think it's best if we step back for a while, Gavin. There's just too much going on for both of us."

His brow furrowed. "But we're just getting to know each other—"

"All the more reason to stop seeing each other now. Why take it any further? Look, we've both got so much baggage—it can't be good for Patrick, or the babies."

"I don't believe this."

"I'm sorry. I'm finding it hard to believe, too." She glanced at her watch and gave him an apologetic glance. "I'm already late for work."

There was one last thing she wanted to do. On instinct, she grabbed his face and kissed him goodbye. Her heart hurt so much she couldn't tell if she'd kissed him too intimately or not, but it was their last kiss and it took all she had not to cry.

He embraced her with strong arms, held her close and kissed her back as if he was trying to change her mind.

But they were at work and this was a public stairwell.

She pulled back. He resisted letting her go, so she gently pushed and gingerly twisted from his grasp.

"I'm sorry," she said, as she raced up the last three stairs to the door.

It had taken Beth most of the last hour to recover. While preoccupied with transferring orders to a chart, the clinic phone rang. It was Jillian.

"You'll never guess what's going on down here. Gavin just got admitted to the ER in full anaphylaxis."

Her heart dropped to the floor, along with the phone receiver. Her stomach went queasy and tears threatened her, making her eyes sting. She raced out the door and called over her shoulder to the other nurse, "Please take over. I've got to go!"

Oh, God. The allergy shots had been too much for him. She swiped at her tears. Blood made a quick exodus from her head as her nurse's training forced its way into her brain—the reaction link between ragweed and cantaloupe sensitivity. The kiss!

When she reached the emergency department, she remembered she didn't know the entry code. Through the window, the room bustled with activity, personnel rushing back and forth. Carmen noticed her, looking frazzled and beyond concerned.

She met Beth at the door. "Listen, things are crazy right now. As soon as I know anything, I'll fill you in. He's OK. But really messed up." She didn't invite Beth in.

The ER door closed and she stood stunned for several more guilt-ridden seconds. Between his festering weed shots and her Tuscan cantaloupe kiss, she could have pushed him over the edge to anaphylaxis with oral-allergy syndrome. Oh, God.

As if she were a zombie, she returned to her department and opened the double doors to find Dr Mehta striding toward her, slipping on her white coat. "I've been summoned to the ER. I'm doing a stat consult."

Beth nodded, knowing exactly where the doctor was going, wondering if she'd almost killed the man she loved. She silently prayed that Gavin would survive.

Unable to face clinic patients right then, she went to the department chartroom where she paced, worried, and prayed more. She found Gavin's chart and looked up his RAST blood tests. There it was, cantaloupe, as positive as any reaction could get. She tamped down the panic and anxiety that threatened to overtake her, and forced herself to keep positive thoughts. He'll be OK. He'll be OK. He's in good hands. They caught it soon enough. Oh, God, did they catch the reaction soon enough? Personal experience warned her that the anaphylactic reaction could go either way, and timing was the key. Thank God he'd been on his way back to the ER after she'd kissed him.

Once Bupinder returned from the ED, Beth went to her office. She stood just outside the door and waited until the doctor noticed her. Dr Mehta lifted large, nearly black eyes and, reading the worry on Beth's face, invited her in.

Beth entered the cluttered office and sat on the edge of the chair across from the desk. She cleared her throat. "How is Gavin?"

"He is doing as well as can be expected for such an unfortunate incident." She placed one hand on the other and put both on top of her paperwork. "If he'd had his EpiPen with him, as was supposed to, he might have avoided this horrid reaction." Bupinder questioned Beth with a confused look. "What is it with these men? They don't think they can die?" She gave a reassuring smile. "But he will survive. They inserted an airway before his throat swelled too much. And he is already doing much better."

The doctor tried to reassure her, but it only forced the knife of guilt deeper into Beth's side.

"One more question?"

"Of course."

"Theoretically speaking," Beth said, "could someone go into anaphylaxis from kissing? Um, that is, if one person had recently eaten something that the other was severely allergic to?"

"Yes. It *is* possible. Microscopic food particles can be passed from mouth to mouth through the saliva, setting off an abnormal release of histamine in the tissues of the allergic person."

"As though the person had eaten the food himself?" Beth closed her eyes and felt tears sneak past her lids. "I mean, herself?" Hell, she'd almost killed him!

"Gavin has been remiss about taking antihistamines before the injections and carrying an EpiPen. I just interviewed him. Remember? This incident didn't have to happen at all. But it is no one's fault, OK?" Knowing eyes glanced across the desk.

"OK," Beth replied, dying to find him and apologize.

* * *

Beth called the ER at 4:15 p.m. and Carmen asked her to come down.

Practically running the whole way, she abruptly slowed and approached Gavin's room in the ER with trepidation. Carmen intercepted her by rushing up to her, a worried look in her eyes. She touched Beth's arm with icy fingers. "Patrick's gone missing."

A jolt of shock stopped Beth in her tracks. "What?"

"The carpool mother, June, dropped him off at home like she always does. I called and told Patrick his daddy had a bad allergy attack and he'd have to stay overnight in the hospital. I told him I'd be over to pick him up as soon as I could get there and to wait for the babysitter." Carmen stared intently into Beth's eyes, and without thinking Beth reached for her hands and held them tightly. "Lauren, the high-school girl from next door, always comes over at four to help him with his homework and watch him until Gav gets home from work. She just called to say Patrick isn't home."

"Oh, my God! I'll go look for him."

Carmen reached in her pocket and tossed Beth something. "Here are the house keys." Strain furrowed her brow. "I wish I could go with you."

"Don't worry. I'll find him. Just take good care of Gavin."

Carmen loved Gavin like a kid brother and Patrick as if he were her own nephew. She glanced at Beth. Their eyes met and Beth could swear she saw a glimmer of respect in Carmen's intense brown stare. Beth flew out of the emergency department, feeling every second of the clock was her enemy keeping her from finding Patrick.

She thought of every possibility of where the boy might be on the drive to Gavin's house. She called the babysitter and asked her to call all of his closest and new friends. Lauren, the sitter, met her at the curb, saying no one knew where he was. They optimistically barreled through the front door, expecting to find Patrick, the whole thing having been a misunderstanding or a boyish joke.

He'd obviously come home, just like the carpool mom had said. An empty bowl of cereal with a few drops of leftover milk sat on the kitchen counter.

Beth and Lauren stormed into his bedroom. He was nowhere to be found. He'd changed out of his school clothes and had left them on his bed. His backpack was gone. The closet door was half-open.

Beth peeked inside. The hamsters weren't in their cages, and the plastic travel ball was missing. A thought popped into her mind. "Is there a pet store anywhere nearby?"

"Yeah. Marvin's Menagerie is about two blocks away."

"Close enough to walk to?"

"Yeah."

"Stay here. I'm going to check it out."

Beth drove fast but carefully to the store and parked out front at five minutes to five, then rushed through the door. She entered to hear the old man behind the counter say, "We're closing in a few minutes."

Long aisles of shelves stacked with cages lined the walls. Squawks and screeches interrupted her thoughts. Animal smells overcame the stench of harsh cleaning agents.

"Have you seen a little boy with brown hair, about this high?" She used her hand to indicate Patrick's height.

"Beth!" Patrick's voice came from further back in the store.

She rushed to him and they hugged. "Why didn't you tell anyone where you'd gone?"

Patrick had changed into his purple and gold Lakers jersey—his courage shirt. He stood next to a cage where Muffy and Puff were harbored. "I needed to say goodbye."

The silver-haired store clerk looked at Beth. "The boy asked me to keep his hamsters for him. I said I'd try to find them a new home. I didn't realize no one knew where he was."

Tears brimmed in her eyes as she realized the sacrifice the boy was about to make for his father. Her heart stung with the knowledge that Patrick thought his father was allergic to his hamsters and felt responsible for his anaphylaxis. She swiped at her eyes.

"Patrick, honey, your father isn't allergic to hamsters. I tested him a couple of weeks ago."

The boy's head popped up. "He's not allergic to them?"

"No." She shook her head.

His tear-swollen eyes peered at her in sheer and ecstatic relief.

She cleared her throat, unable to remove the swell of emotion from her voice. "This is what happens when we keep secrets. I should never have agreed. Because you didn't tell your father, you've had to carry around a burden that must have been unbearable. And, worse, you almost gave your hamsters away because of it."

"I know."

"If you'd been honest, and told your dad what worried you, none of this would have been necessary."

The boy nodded his head with a pained expression.

"Excuse me, folks, but it's closing time."

"Sure. OK," Beth said, standing up. "Thanks for taking care of Patrick and the hamsters. But we'll take them back home where they belong."

"Let me get you a couple of travel boxes. Those Goldens fight when they're in the same cage."

Patrick cracked a knowing smile. "I know." He picked up his yellow plastic see-through ball and handed it to Beth. Relief smoothed the lines of his forehead. They walked outside, holding the hamsters and each other's hands.

"Promise me you'll never pull another stunt like this again. I don't know what your father would do without you."

"I promise."

They got into her car and she buckled the boy into the backseat. Before she started the car she called Carmen and then Lauren. When she pulled out into traffic, Beth looked at Patrick in the rear-view mirror and smiled. "Let's take the hamsters home, then go see your dad."

By the time they arrived at Mercy Hospital, things had calmed down considerably in the ED.

Now stable, Gavin had been moved to the holding area for overnight observation.

Beth delivered Patrick to Gavin's side. He grew shy after seeing Gavin's puffy, red-blotched face. Beth rubbed his shoulder and urged him closer.

"Hey, buddy?" Gavin said. "You gave me a fright."

Patrick wasn't the only one handing out fright that day. Gavin could have died, and it was Beth's fault.

"I'm sorry, Dad." Gavin pulled Patrick closer for a hug. He looked at Beth, as though just noticing she was in the room, and mouthed "Thank you." After their meeting and breakup in the stairwell earlier, she wasn't sure if she should stick around or not. But she wanted to make sure Patrick finally told his father the truth and that they would sort things out before she left.

"I was so *scared* when Carmen said you got sick. I thought it was my fault." Patrick gave a cough. Twice. The boy either needed his inhaler or he was shaken up by his father's appearance and it was a nervous bark.

"I'm fine, Patrick." They'd removed the airway and Gavin could talk again. He sounded as though he'd been smoking cigarettes his entire life. "My allergy shots were too much for me." He pulled away from the boy to look into his eyes. "Why would this be your fault?"

"Because of my hamsters."

"What hamsters?" Gavin glanced Beth's way, first a question then understanding dawning on his face.

"My secret hamsters. I thought you were allergic, just like our cat Tommy. I thought I made you sick." The boy burst into tears and Gavin held him close.

"No. You didn't make me sick, but you should never have kept a secret from me."

"I know," the boy sobbed.

Gavin rubbed Patrick's head. "Listen, buddy, it's you and me. No matter what, we'll always have each other. I'll take care of my allergies, and you won't ever keep a secret or run away again. OK?"

"OK, Dad."

As obvious as the smell in Marvin's Menagerie,

a thought occurred to Beth. The poor man had a responsibility to his son *right now*. They'd steam-rollered into each other's lives and she'd thrown him curve ball after curveball.

Patrick had promised to tell Gavin about his secret pets, and Beth had assumed their fishing trip would have been the perfect time. Instead, she'd deceived Gavin by not telling him in the first place.

What kind of a mom would she make? She'd colluded with a nine-year-old boy over secret hamsters, and look at all the trouble it had caused. The boy had run away and any number of horrible things could have happened to him. Just thinking of the possibilities made her feel ill. If she were Gavin, she'd never speak to her again.

The whole mess was her fault—anaphylaxis from the kiss, running away because of the secret. Gavin and Patrick deserved more time and plenty of space to regroup and heal, and the Riordan boys would be much better off without her.

Reassured that Gavin was fine, Beth backed away from the ER cubicle and turned to leave.

She saw Carmen on her way out. "I don't want to disturb them any more. Patrick needs time alone with his dad."

Carmen nodded in understanding.

"By the way, I think Patrick needs his inhaler. Could you make sure he takes a puff or two?"

"Will do."

She'd made the right decision to break things off. Between Gavin getting her pregnant and her almost killing him, they'd proved to be hazardous to each other's health. She loved him, but that was a different matter. Keeping it real, at this moment, Patrick needed a father more than Gavin needed a pregnant girlfriend.

CHAPTER ELEVEN

BETH taped the last box, lifted it and piled it on top of the others in her living room. The modest-sized apartment had never felt more cramped. Speaking of cramped, her muscles would pay later for all of the packing, bending and lifting. She used her palms to massage her lower back, which had been hurting more each day.

Today marked the beginning of her second trimester. She'd never gotten this far in a pregnancy before. She smiled ruefully and shook her head. Life was so damn crazy.

Jillian came lumbering down the short hall with a dust smudge on her cheek and her red hair flagrantly misbehaving. She held a cardboard box in one arm and a lamp in the other. "Where should I put this?"

"Oh. Leave the lamp where it is. I'll need it tonight."

"OK, boss." Jillian smiled and made an about-face.

Jillian had helped her get through the past two weeks and, eternally grateful, Beth wondered how she would have survived without her friendship. When she'd cried until she'd thought she'd vomit after making the hardest decision of her life—to stay away from Gavin and Patrick—Jillian had been there. When she'd cursed life for not working out the way she thought it should have, Jillian had listened to her rant. When she'd curled up into a ball, depressed over her decision to move in with her mom to help save money, Jillian had made sure she'd eaten and had held her hand so she hadn't felt alone.

Friends like Jillian and men like Gavin only came along once in a lifetime.

Moving in with Ruth was a small sacrifice for

the sake of the babies. But the decision had taken its toll, and today, when Beth should have been celebrating the beginning of her second trimester, she felt weary.

She surveyed the room. Lila stretched across the back of the only remaining chair, eyes squinting, the tip of her tail flicking and betraying her discontent. "Oh, get over it. Ruth loves you."

Would *Beth* be any happier than her cat, moving back with her mother to a house one step away from the demolition ball? How had everything gotten so messed up?

Lifting another box, Beth felt moisture between her legs. Realizing she'd been holding back too long, she needed to use the bathroom.

Gavin walked Patrick to the ER, feeling bad the boy would have to spend another Saturday in the Mercy Hospital doctors' lounge. But that was the reality of being a single father. He glanced up in time to see a wild-maned redhead running for the entrance. Jillian.

"I need a wheelchair," she said.

He looked around for the usual left-behind wheelchairs but found nothing in view. "What's wrong?"

She went still, her wide green eyes betraying her alarm. "Beth's bleeding."

"Where is she?"

"She's in the car."

"Let's go," he said, racing behind her.

Bleeding? The babies. A jolt of fear slammed into his chest. He wanted those babies as much as she did.

Patrick tried to keep up. "Is Beth all right?"

In the car Gavin saw Beth crumpled over her lap, her hands over her ears, sobbing. His heart wrenched at the sight.

"Stay there, Patrick," he said to his son trying his best to sound calm. He turned and directed Jillian. "Call Dr Scott to meet us in the ER." He handed her his cellphone.

Gavin knelt beside Beth. "Come on, sweetheart. Let me help you get up."

"I can't go through this again," she whimpered. She removed her hands from her head and glanced at Gavin, her face contorted with sorrow.

It finally clicked why she'd pushed him away—no man had ever stood by her when it had counted. Well, at this most crucial time he was not about to let the woman he loved down.

"We'll do whatever it takes to save these babies, Beth. I promise." He reached for her hands. "Come on, now, let me help you up."

She gazed gratefully into his eyes as he lifted her to her feet. The air caught in his chest from touching her again.

Patrick rushed to her and threw his arms around her neck. Tears squeezed from her eyes when she hugged him back.

"I don't want you to be sick," Patrick said.

"Thank you, sweetheart. That means so much to me."

Gavin realized Patrick was crying, too, and his heart clenched at the sight of the two people he loved most in the world holding and consoling each other.

"Are you in any pain?" Gavin asked.

"No. Just my back from all the lifting I've been doing."

"You're not cramping?"

She shook her head. "I just have to go to the bathroom all the time."

Gavin didn't wait for a wheelchair to appear out of thin air. He lifted Beth up, and for the second time in two months carried her through the emergency department doors in his arms.

"We need a room. Now," Gavin said to Carmen as he rushed by.

Carmen pointed to room four, and Gavin made a beeline for it.

Beth took comfort in his arms, and having him near helped her quell the fear roiling inside her. More tears leaked out when she considered the possibility of another miscarriage. As if he could read her mind, he gently placed her on the ER gurney and cupped her face with his warm hands.

"We'll do whatever it takes to stop the bleeding, then I'll bring you home and take care of you."

"Gavin, what if—?"

He placed a finger over her mouth to stop her from saying what she feared most. "We're not going to let that happen."

He paced back and forth on the other side of the curtain while she undressed and put on the exam gown. Then he made sure she was covered to her chin with a hospital blanket. He sat on the edge of the bed and patted her hand, looking sure and confident.

She loved him for that. For being strong when she wanted to fall apart. But, then, she'd loved him all along.

"You OK?" he asked, jumping to the sink and dampening a cloth.

"I'm not in pain, if that's what you mean."

"Yeah. Well, that's something." He sounded optimistic as he dabbed at her forehead with the cool cloth. "I'm glad you're not in pain." He glanced into her eyes and briefly she could see the worry and fear he'd been hiding from her.

Karen appeared with Carmen at her side. Both looked concerned. "What's going on?" Karen asked.

Gavin explained everything.

Carmen did a quick temperature check. "Low-grade fever," she noted, before applying the blood-pressure cuff.

"I want a urine sample. Then I'll do a pelvic exam. If necessary, I'll do an ultrasound."

"Could you do one regardless?" Gavin asked.

Karen nodded.

Gavin glanced at Beth as if asking whether he should leave while the doctor examined her. She could tell he wanted to stay. She didn't want him to leave either, so she grabbed his hand for support before she lay back and put her feet in the stirrups. His grip was tight, and tension poured from his eyes. Rather than stare at the ceiling, she watched Gavin. He smiled reassuringly, but she noticed a tiny twitch at the corner of one eye.

When Karen had finished her examination, she removed her gloves and cleared her throat. "The bleeding doesn't appear to be coming from the cervix. Have you had any burning when you urinate?"

Beth shook her head.

"I suspect the bleeding is nothing more than a whopping case of cystitis. I can treat that easily enough with an antibiotic that won't harm the babies." She folded her arms and looked over the exam table. "You do seem to be showing early and minimal signs of dilatation of the cervix, though."

Beth's heart dropped. How could she bring twins to full term if her cervix was already opening?

"What do you mean?" Gavin spoke up.

"She may have what we call an incompetent cervix. It's the cause of a quarter of second trimester losses."

Beth's hand shot up to cover her eyes, and she groaned with the horrible news that her cervix was weak. Was that why she'd miscarried twice before?

"It's not the end of the world, Beth. I can watch you closely and, if necessary, we can do a cerclage."

"Stitch my cervix closed?"

The doctor nodded and patted Beth's hip to tell her she could put her legs down. "It's 85 to 90 percent successful."

Gavin extended the exam table so she'd have something to put her feet on while she shimmied back up the bed.

"Before we go to that extreme, I want to see how things progress. The bleeding will clear up as we treat the urinary tract infection. But if, over the next few weeks, the cervix dilates to 2.5 centimeters, we'll need to take action. In the meantime, I'm putting you on bedrest for the next week and restricted activity for the remainder of your pregnancy. We want these twins to stay in the womb as long as possible."

So did Gavin. He cleared his throat. Karen glanced at him. "About that ultrasound? I'd like to see our kids."

Relief washed over Beth, and hope replaced the dread she'd been feeling earlier. She'd worry about the logistics of the bedrest orders later.

Our kids. She glanced at Gavin. He looked far more relaxed and smiled without the nervous eye twitch. She beamed from the depths of her heart.

Gavin reached for her hand again, and held on tight.

Karen prepared to leave the exam room. "I'll go and write up the orders and be back with a prescription. And after we do the ultrasound, I'll make an appointment to see you next week in my office."

Beth nodded. Gavin leaned over as if to kiss her, but he stopped abruptly. "You haven't eaten any cantaloupe, have you?"

Through tears of joy and love, she laughed. "Not today." On a sudden, serious note she needed to know one more thing. "Can you ever forgive me for keeping Patrick's secret from you?"

"Of course. I can't thank you enough for finding him that day."

She rubbed her stomach and dropped her head back on the gurney. "I want to be a mother with all of my heart, Gavin."

"And you're going to make a great mom—I've seen you in action with Patrick, remember?"

He had faith in her.

She looked into Gavin's warm gaze, then admired his strong jaw and the sexy cleft in his chin, and grinned. "You're going to make a great dad, too."

His eyes came to rest on hers as he grew serious. "I promise to always be here for you and our kids, Bethany. I can't imagine life without you."

A burst of tingles warmed her heart. Overwhelmed with emotion, she took a deep breath but couldn't find her voice.

"One more thing," he said.

"Yes?" She barely made a sound.

"I've put this off long enough. I kept thinking I'd find the perfect time or place because I wanted it to be special when I told you, but look where it's gotten us. From one ER visit to another."

"What are you talking about?"

His earth-brown eyes blazed into hers. "I love you, Bethany."

Her heart stumbled over the next few beats. "I love you, too, Gavin."

He bent and softly kissed her. Something broke inside and she let go of every doubt and fear she'd hoarded over the past three months. They would make it work. He'd promised to be there for her and he was a man of his word. She believed it to her core.

Kissing Gavin, she knew they were meant to be together, and she'd never felt more positive about anything in her life.

EPILOGUE

BETH stretched out on the chaise longue in Gavin's master bedroom, listening to the bustle in the house. Restless and eager to be taken off bedrest orders, she sipped the herbal iced tea Gavin had served her. Just one more day.

"Put that over there," he instructed the movers. "Oh, and that can go in the extra bedroom down the hall."

Patrick rushed in with a huge smile and a clear plastic ball with a hamster in it. He put it on the floor, grabbed the other hamster from his cargo shorts pocket and thrust it her way. "Here's Muffy."

She grinned and welcomed both Patrick and the rodent into her arms. They snuggled together.

He glanced up to her with adoring eyes. "I'm glad you're all better."

"Me, too. But I'll be even happier when I can get off my duff."

"What's a duff?"

"My backside."

"You mean your butt?" He giggled.

She nodded and tickled her chin with Muffy's silky fur. Lila made eye contact from across the room, then rushed outside when Puff rolled toward her in the transparent yellow ball.

"Your poor dad's going to have to live on antihistamines with all these animals around here."

"He doesn't care. He loves us."

She smiled and nodded at the beautiful direct logic of a nine-year-old boy confident in his father's love. "Yeah. He does."

"Are the babies OK?"

They'd finally told Patrick about his future siblings and he seemed cautiously curious.

"Dr Scott says so, and I feel much better so I say, yes, the babies are fine."

Gavin entered with a tray of sandwiches. "I just

got off the phone with my contact. Your mother is officially on the shortlist at Sunset Palms and they plan to open the new wing next month."

"That's wonderful! I can't wait to tell her."

"I already have, and when I told her the place came highly recommended by my grandmother, she sounded excited."

"Really?"

"Hey," he said, putting down the tray and lifting his palms with a shrug. "It's me. Would I lie?"

She shook her head, loving the cocky side of her man.

"And when you're ready to go back to work, there's a great part-time position available as a triage nurse in the ER. In case you're interested."

"Gavin, I've already got a job in Allergy."

"Doctor says you can't work full time, remember?"

"Maybe the allergy department can accommodate me?"

"Of course they'd try, but Bupinder needs a full-time nurse. It wouldn't be fair."

He sat beside her on the narrow lounger. "You

won't have to do lifting or bedside care. You won't even have to stand for long periods of time. You'll just assess the walk-in patients, take their vital signs and history, and decide if they belong in the ER or in Urgent Care. And sometimes, when people are having a really rough time, you can comfort the family members. You're perfect for the job. And did I mention it's only four hours three days a week?"

She took the wet cloth he offered, wiped her hands, and quickly thought things through. She should still be able to counsel patients at the teen clinic, and why couldn't she continue to deliver dinners for Senior Nutrition for a few more months? All Karen meant by restricted activity for the rest of the pregnancy was resting for a few hours each day and avoiding heavy lifting and cutting back on work. She'd talk to Bupinder before she made her final decision.

Since Gavin had asked her to move in with him and Patrick, she'd be around for the boy when he got home from school when it started again in September. Maureen had decided to spend another semester in Oxford—she'd even found a job there. Things were definitely looking up.

Gavin wolfed down a sandwich and jumped up to rummage through the top drawer of his dresser. "There's something I need to show you." He produced what he was looking for.

"Your EpiPen?"

"I've got to set a good example for my son. Hey," he said to Patrick, waving the container, "have you taken your inhalers today?"

"Yup. Did you take your antihistamine?"

Gavin grinned. "Sure did. Listen, sport, could you give us a minute alone?"

Patrick rolled his eyes. "Are you gonna kiss her again?"

"Maybe. If I get lucky."

Patrick took Muffy from Beth's lap and toed the rolling ball toward the door. "Can I have a sandwich?"

"Of course, but wash your hands first."

Once he'd left, Gavin repeated, "Like I said, I've got to set a good example for my kids."

"With your EpiPen?" she reiterated.

He tapped his temple with his finger. "You only think it's an EpiPen." He chuckled and sat next to her on the chaise longue, again. "When my grandmother left me this house, it was her way to ensure my happiness. So she gave me another gift to go along with it." He opened the empty cigar-shaped cylinder and carefully tapped something out. A dainty gold ring with a delicate diamond popped into his hand. He held it up for Beth's inspection. "This belonged to my grandmother. She wore it until the day she died." He pressed his forehead to hers and gazed into her eyes. "There's an old custom in the Riordan clan. You almost killed me, so you have to marry me."

She rubbed noses with him. "Not exactly the romantic proposal I've always dreamed about, but I like where you're going with this idea."

"I love you, and I want to marry you, Bethany. Before we become parents." The simple sincerity in his eyes took her breath away.

She brushed his lips with her own and stared into his gorgeous dark-eyed gaze, eyes she longed to see every day for the rest of her life.

"Your idea definitely has merit, Dr Riordan, but…" She gave him another lingering kiss. "My relatives have a tradition, too. They say all great decisions take time and consideration." She wrapped her arms around his neck, pulled him closer and kissed him again. She'd never grow tired of his warm, soft lips. Finally, she broke away, a mischievous twinkle in her eyes. "But when have I ever listened to them?" She grinned and nuzzled his cheek with her nose. "Especially where you're concerned."

"Is that a yes, Bethany?"

A smile tickled across her lips. "Most definitely. Yes."

MEDICAL™

―∿――― *Large Print* ―∿―
Titles for the next six months…

March

SHEIKH SURGEON CLAIMS HIS BRIDE Josie Metcalfe
A PROPOSAL WORTH WAITING FOR   Lilian Darcy
A DOCTOR, A NURSE: A LITTLE MIRACLE Carol Marinelli
TOP-NOTCH SURGEON, PREGNANT NURSE Amy Andrews
A MOTHER FOR HIS SON   Gill Sanderson
THE PLAYBOY DOCTOR'S MARRIAGE   Fiona Lowe
PROPOSAL

April

A BABY FOR EVE   Maggie Kingsley
MARRYING THE MILLIONAIRE DOCTOR   Alison Roberts
HIS VERY SPECIAL BRIDE   Joanna Neil
CITY SURGEON, OUTBACK BRIDE   Lucy Clark
A BOSS BEYOND COMPARE   Dianne Drake
THE EMERGENCY DOCTOR'S   Molly Evans
CHOSEN WIFE

May

DR DEVEREUX'S PROPOSAL   Margaret McDonagh
CHILDREN'S DOCTOR,   Meredith Webber
MEANT-TO-BE WIFE
ITALIAN DOCTOR, SLEIGH-BELL BRIDE Sarah Morgan
CHRISTMAS AT WILLOWMERE   Abigail Gordon
DR ROMANO'S CHRISTMAS BABY   Amy Andrews
THE DESERT SURGEON'S SECRET SON   Olivia Gates

MILLS & BOON®
Pure reading pleasure™

0209 LP 2P P1 Medical

MEDICAL™

Large Print

June

A MUMMY FOR CHRISTMAS	Caroline Anderson
A BRIDE AND CHILD WORTH WAITING FOR	Marion Lennox
ONE MAGICAL CHRISTMAS	Carol Marinelli
THE GP'S MEANT-TO-BE BRIDE	Jennifer Taylor
THE ITALIAN SURGEON'S CHRISTMAS MIRACLE	Alison Roberts
CHILDREN'S DOCTOR, CHRISTMAS BRIDE	Lucy Clark

July

THE GREEK DOCTOR'S NEW-YEAR BABY	Kate Hardy
THE HEART SURGEON'S SECRET CHILD	Meredith Webber
THE MIDWIFE'S LITTLE MIRACLE	Fiona McArthur
THE SINGLE DAD'S NEW-YEAR BRIDE	Amy Andrews
THE WIFE HE'S BEEN WAITING FOR	Dianne Drake
POSH DOC CLAIMS HIS BRIDE	Anne Fraser

August

CHILDREN'S DOCTOR, SOCIETY BRIDE	Joanna Neil
THE HEART SURGEON'S BABY SURPRISE	Meredith Webber
A WIFE FOR THE BABY DOCTOR	Josie Metcalfe
THE ROYAL DOCTOR'S BRIDE	Jessica Matthews
OUTBACK DOCTOR, ENGLISH BRIDE	Leah Martyn
SURGEON BOSS, SURPRISE DAD	Janice Lynn

 MILLS & BOON®
Pure reading pleasure™

0209 LP 2P P2 Medical